I0653826

The Ink Slingers Guild

Presents

BENT HORIZONS

A Collection of Short Stories
Volume Four

Contributing Authors

Nicole DragonBeck

Dee Rea

JM Paquette

Dalia Lance

Desiree Matlock

Anne Cargile

Alanna J. Rubin

Erika Lance

Lisa Barry

Rhiannon Matlock

Laura Price

Witching Hour Publishing, Inc.

Witching Hour Publishing, Inc.

ISBN-10: 1943121079
ISBN-13: 978-1-943121-07-6

Ink Slingers Guild crest: Nicole DragonBeck
Ink Slingers Guild crest digital artistry: Desi Matlock
Cover Design: Lisa Barry
Editor: Courtenay Dodds www.CourtenayDodds.com

Introduction

The Ink Slingers Guild is a group of writers who come together for support and encouragement. We give each other inspiration and the occasional kick in the arse.

This collection of short stories is based on a writing exercise done at every ISG meeting. The exercise is to have three members each pick one word. Members have five minutes to compose a story with the chosen words. As with any creative outlet, members take each other into new worlds the way only writers can.

And the concept of these books was born.

Bent Horizons is the Ink Slinger's fourth anthology based on that exercise. As with the first anthology, ***Beyond the Threshold***, the second, ***Into the Abyss***, and the third, ***On the Verge***, the authors had several months to create their stories.

The words that were chosen this year were:

- Glisten
- Titillating
- Horizon

Each story is an adventure, so sit back and enjoy as the Ink Slingers Guild brings you to their **Bent Horizons**.

www.InkSlingersGuild.com

Dedication

For the Dreamer. Never stop dreaming, never stop creating and don't let anyone or anything get in the way of your goals.

Cheers!

Contents

Blood Oath

By Nicole DragonBeck

Shanaye Barry looked at the envelope in her hand, and what it contained. With bloodless fingers, her other hand gripped the locket at her throat. In seconds, her world had been turned upside down, inside out, ripped apart and put back together *a la* Frankenstein.

No one should have the power to ruin a person's concept of their existence with just a photograph, Shan thought with unaccustomed bitterness.

Just half an hour before, it had been another normal day. On the way to see a movie with Brie, Corrine, Josh, and William, friends and fellow freshmen at County Kirk Community College, they stopped at an old gas station for snacks to smuggle into the theater. A small notice tacked in the corner of the window came into focus with enough force to knock the breath out of her lungs and pull her from her favorite daydream.

The words were titillating, calling her, commanding her to read. When she tried to, they swam in front of her eyes, but she managed to make out part of the meaning.

Seeking qualified personnel for exciting and gsedjfoin career opportuapjpoijne. Special training mmcojnwoi. Apply within. Akjjviojoab akdjhf read this sign.

It had been intriguing, partly because it was written in a language she had never seen before, but mostly because when she looked harder, the words melted into meaningless scribbles.

Shan glanced down at what she held and tried not to stare at the photo. It could be doctored, but if it weren't...?

When she had gone inside the Kwik Mart and asked the lanky, dark-haired guy at the counter what the advertisement had been about, a flash of surprise preceded a quick phone call, then a door had appeared, literally *appeared out of thin air*. Shan had been pushed through without so much as a by your leave.

Before she had time to be worried about what her friends

would think and the fact she didn't have anyone to pay ransom for her, a voice had welcomed her, told her she had entered something called a Space-Time Warp with memory-wiping wards for anyone not expressly invited, and ordered her to sit.

Shan's eyes stole back to the envelope, then darted away to the nondescript walls of the dimly lit conference room. It was sparsely occupied. Most of the chairs around the oval table were empty. Twelve were not. A woman in a military uniform stood behind a podium, watching the other occupants study their respective envelopes.

From the expressions on their faces, everyone had found something as unsettling as Shan had. Military Woman's first words echoed in Shan's head. *I will need you to broaden the horizons of your minds in order to accept what I am about to tell you. Some of you will not believe me. It is true nonetheless.*

Shan looked at the photo. It showed a young boy, not yet two years old. His face, that had Shan's round cheeks, the same face that was trapped in Shan's locket, was lit up in a beam of delight. He leaned over an ornate fountain with a rapt expression, his hand outstretched. Beside him, sitting on the edge of the fountain, was a wispy figure with too-long limbs and long silver hair. On a level that went beyond memory or instinct, Shan recognized both of them, and it frightened and thrilled her.

Shan's hand rose of its own volition, as if she were back in elementary school, drawing all eyes to her, and her mouth spoke before she could stop it.

"None of this can be real."

"Oh?" Military Woman said.

"It was a closed adoption," Shan tried to explain. "The records are sealed. And there is no such thing as Fairy. It's...scientifically impossible!"

"Miss Barry," Military Woman said with a smile. "Science is overrated."

"So these fairies are trying to get into our world and take over, and they're using people like..." Shan almost choked on the words, "...like me who can see their magic to do it?"

"Yes."

Shan's eyes flicked to the enlarged advertisement behind

the podium, and the way the words morphed. The fact that she could read more of its message than anyone else besides the latecomer gave some credence to Military Woman's story, that it was in the language of Fairy and only those who had Fairy blood could decipher the meaning, and those with stronger ties to that part of them could read more.

Her eyes flicked back to the latecomer. He had not taken a seat at the table, instead remaining standing in the back corner. A dark goatee framed his petulant mouth and dark hair covered his ears. His slouch made him appear shorter than he was, one hand in the pocket of his worn jeans, the other dangling his envelope.

"How did you get this photo?" Shan asked, shoving the photo back in her envelope.

"There are Doors," Military Woman said. "Ways to move into that world. It's too complicated to explain..."

"Try," Shan demanded.

"Miss Barry, would you ask a nuclear physicist to explain the entirety of molecular phenomena in three minutes after you saw an atomic bomb go off? Would you be satisfied with the explanation he gave? Let me assure you, *all* your questions will be answered, just not here and now."

"If you knew about this, how could you let that happen?" Shan said, the first stirring of anger tightening in her stomach.

"There are only so many of us out there. This operation is privately funded through a trust left by its founder, Mr. Herbert Sanders. It takes time to find the people who have the qualifications we require."

"And what qualifications would that be?"

It was the guy with the goatee who spoke.

"Every person in this room can see the Doors I mentioned."

"And you know this because of that sign?" Goatee asked.

"That is correct."

Goatee nodded and held up his photo. "And why this?"

"To impress upon you the nature and M.O. of the enemy." Military Woman addressed the whole group, "You are the only ones who can do something about the threat to our world. Think about what you've learned here today, and in twenty-four hours, I'll expect to hear from you. I realize that is not much time, and this is not a decision to be made lightly, but the fate of *all* is at stake. Please return to your respective doors, they will open momentarily and send you home."

Shan turned in a daze, her mind registering that a door had reappeared in the wall. A man in dark glasses and a uniform held open the door. Shan stepped through without thinking and found herself in the Kwik Mart, staring at a refrigerator behind the counter, William and Josh behind her, their arms full of snacks.

"So? Are you going to stand there staring at the soda all day or can we go?" Josh said, nodding towards the cashier. "He's finished ringing up, and we're going to be be late for the movie. Honestly, with you people it's like herding a clowder of cats!"

"No, we can go," Shan said, tucking the envelope into her shirt so they wouldn't see it.

The cashier winked at her as she walked out.

***

Shan begged out of the movie, saying she suddenly felt ill, which wasn't entirely a lie. She *did* feel like she'd just woken up from a night spent downing a large quantity of whiskey sours. Her mind wasn't connecting thoughts in the right order.

She had gotten her life on track. She had a plan. She was going somewhere. Why had this happened, and why now? *But you always hoped one he'd come find you, when you were both a little older and a lot wiser,* a voice reminded her as she lay in bed, playing with the locket.

She sighed. Having spent her childhood in the foster system, she knew what it was like to wonder about the people who had dropped you in this world and left you alone in it, even if they left because a semi-trailer had flattened their car.

Giving the baby up for adoption hadn't been easy, and it hadn't felt good, but she'd done the best thing she could for him and washed her hands of the whole thing. Now someone wanted her to get her hands dirty again. She tried using the same logic she had used when deciding whether to give him up for adoption: what would I want somebody in *my* position to do for me if I was in *that* position?

She was being manipulated. She *knew* it. It made thinking difficult. What was she supposed to do? Looking at the photo made up Shan's mind. *I got him into this mess, I should at least do something to get him out. Though,* she noted, *he did look oddly happy.*

Perhaps the fairies abhorred the idea of hurting children as much as humans generally did, but as soon as he was old enough, he was fair game for whatever plot they had concocted. It occurred to her that she didn't know his name.

In the envelope was a list of things that were recommended she pack, and another even longer list of things prohibited. It took less than an hour to pack, and slightly longer to make up a story about needing some time to find herself, which left her friends more confused than enlightened.

The next day Shan biked to the gas station. It was now deserted, with "For Rent" signs over the windows. Inside there was only slightly more evidence of life.

"I knew you'd come back," a lazy drawl greeted her. "It's in the eyes. You get to know these things."

It was the cashier, except now he wore a dark suit, and had an ear-piece in one ear. He managed to look fairly intimidating despite the youth of his face and the sunglasses resting on his head. He winked.

"Alright, I'm here. What am I supposed to do now?" Shan asked.

"Go on back to the Door. Your escort will meet you on the other side."

"My bike..." Shan started to say.

"It'll be taken care of," the guy smiled. "I'll make sure of it."

Shan nodded. The magically appearing Door led to a different place this time, all concrete and glass in a sci-fi motif that made Shan's skin chafe. *And here I was expecting fairy forests and old stone castles,* Shan thought.

"Ms. Barry?" a crisp voice inquired.

"Yes." Shan turned.

The short, neatly dressed man was balding but his

eyebrows and mustache more than compensated. "Ms. Barry, my name is Jenkins. I will be your guidance counselor for the duration of your training. If you'll follow me, I'll show you to your dormitory and then to the Welcome Luncheon."

Shan nodded and followed the man, who walked with choppy steps, through pristine halls of unforgiving angles and antiseptic gel. Her dormitory was a little better. It, at least, had some color, an insipid yellow of not-quite-dead chrysanthemums. The room was occupied by a pair of double-bunks, four chests and two girls who looked vaguely familiar.

"Top bunks are taken," the red-head chewing gum said at once.

"If you want it, you can have mine," the dark-skinned girl said with a pretty smile.

"Thanks, but you were here first," Shan said, setting her pack on the bottom bed to the right.

"I'm Meg, that's Beatrice," the red-head said, and snapped an impressive bubble. "Pretty wild, huh?"

"Um, yeah," Shan said. "I'm Shan, by the way."

"I know," Meg smiled, pale blue eyes lukewarm as she tossed Shan a folder.

Inside was a tag with Shan's full name on it, a schedule of events that started with a Welcome Luncheon, a small brochure with very strange pictures and tiny captions, and a map of each of the twelve levels of the facility. Off-limits areas were marked with red stripes.

Shan tried not to mind that Meg had read her folder as she examined the schedule. "Do we all have the same?"

Meg shook her head, long hair flying. "For the first couple days, yeah. Intro, meet and greet, testing, but then it's blank. I guess it's a surprise." She waved her hands in mock excitement.

"Testing?" Shan grimaced.

Meg shrugged. "Aptitude, strengths, weaknesses. Nothing painful. I think."

Shan wondered why these two had decided to come back to Unit X, but she didn't want to pry into whatever dark secret had come out of their envelopes. Meg had no such compunction.

"So, why'd you pitch up?" she asked, grinning devilishly.

Shan and Beatrice gave each other uncomfortable looks.

"Oh, come on," Meg said. "My mom died when I was three. Supposedly. Apparently not true, if this is not a game show joke. And it's not like I remember her or anything, but a reunion could be kinda cool, especially if I rescue her in badass style. So? What about you guys?"

A sharp rap on the door saved Shan from answering and brought all three girls to attention.

"Ms. Barry? Ms. Keaton? Ms. O'Neil?"

When Meg opened the door, Jenkins stood there, a politely contrite expression on his face "I'm sorry to disturb you, but it's time for the Welcome..."

"Buffet!" Meg snapped a theatrical salute and breezed past him.

"I was going to say Luncheon Briefing," Jenkins said, bemused.

Beatrice nodded, smiling quietly as she followed Meg. Shan brought up the rear. Jenkins trotted them to a large cafeteria full of round tables. It looked something straight out of a high-school, all plastic and dull metal. Serving banks stood along one side.

"This is the Mess," Jenkins said with a little bow. "All meals are taken here. There is to be *no* food in the Dormitory."

Meg made a face behind his back and Beatrice looked solemn.

"Mess?" Shan whispered as they walked to the back of the very short line.

"Army talk. Basically, it's the dining room," Meg said.

"This is the neatest Mess I've ever seen," Shan said and Meg cracked a genuine smile.

Lunch was laid out. Platters of fruit, tubs of salads and pitchers of dressing were first. Little sandwiches cut into triangles with green and yellow fillings, cheese and cold cuts were next. A variety of pastries ended the selection.

Shan picked up a tray and put some fruit and ham on her plate. She stood by the pastries, deliberating, until someone came up behind her. It was Goatee.

"Sorry," Shan said, grabbing a handful of small biscuits

with pink centers and one of the chocolate things.

"Not a problem," Goatee said. "I'm George."

"Shan," she said, and stood there awkwardly.

He looked pensive, as though he wanted to say more but didn't know how she would take it. The scratching of a microphone announcing the commencement of the Welcome Briefing sent them hurrying to one of the occupied tables in the center. Meg and Beatrice sat together, but the seats next to theirs were already taken. George pulled out a chair for her and then sat beside her.

Shan glanced at her companions, trying to be inconspicuous. Including herself, Meg, Beatrice and George, there were four others: a lanky oriental boy in glasses who looked like he was either twelve or thirty, a blond boy with a shirt that said "What are you Tolkien about?", an almost pretty Hispanic boy with shining curls and large brown eyes, and hulking guy sporting a crew cut and a crooked nose and who looked like he lived and breathed football.

A bright spotlight illuminated Military Woman on the stage. She cleared her throat and began to speak.

"My name is Lieutenant Ferguson." Shan wondered how long it would take for the nickname Fergie to take hold. "I oversee the training in Unit X. You are our eight newest recruits, but in less than eight weeks you will join the honorable ranks of Unit X. Please enjoy your lunch, and then we'll get right on with it."

    ***

After they had eaten, Jenkins and another man Shan didn't know escorted them out of the Mess, down a bright corridor and through a pair of double doors. They found themselves in a classroom, one that would be found in a cheap sci-fi TV show. A podium and a huge screen were set up in the front. The chairs and desks were all silver curves and black highlights, and each one had a metal plate with a name engraved on it. The screen on Shan's desk did nothing when she tapped it experimentally.

The boy in the Tolkien shirt spoke first. "So the schedule says this is Intro. Who wants to go first?"

"I'm Meg. This is Shan, and Beatrice."

"I'm George."

"Dave." The football player.

"Enrique." The Hispanic boy.

"Jonson. Nice to meet you all." The oriental boy.

"And I'm Sil."

"Is that Elvish?" Meg joked, with a pointed look at his shirt.

"Close. It's short for Silmarillion," Sil shrugged. "What can I say - my parents are super-nerds."

"Oh." For once, Meg was speechless.

"At least I'm well prepared for this," Sil quipped. "Have you guys seen the Library?"

Seven heads shook in response.

"It's amazing!" Sil breathed. "All those books you read about the hidden folk, other worlds, elves and magic? Well, they're real accounts of Fae encounters! Fortunately, I've read most of them, but it will probably be a good idea to go over it again."

Meg found a comeback. "Looks like the apple didn't fall far from the tree."

At that moment Major Fergie walked into the room. She pressed a button under her desk and the screens flashed to life in too-bright blue light.

"Good afternoon recruits. Tomorrow, you'll go through Aptitude Testing and Placement, and over the next few weeks you'll go through training necessary to..."

"Weeks?"

Military Woman looked to see who had spoken.

"Sorry," Shan said. "I thought we would be getting into Fairy sooner. What about..."

"Ms. Barry, those weeks will be well spent learning how to not die. Don't worry, the fairies will be there when you're done. Now, I wanted to give you a little history of Unit X. First, are there any questions?"

George's hand shot up. "Why haven't we heard of this before?"

"Excellent question. The simple answer is that it's difficult to find and contact you while being discreet, and that's all I can tell you until you get higher clearance."

"Are we going into combat?" Dave the football player asked.

"That depends on the results of your Testing. Not everyone is cut out for combat. There are many posts that need manning in this operation: medical, tactical, liaison, and counter-intelligence."

Shan raised her hand, phrasing the question in innocuous terms. "So when *do* we get into Fairy?"

"Yeah!" Sil seconded with enthusiasm.

"Ah, yes, the atomic physicist," Lt. Fergie said. "The answer to that is you don't. Hopping between worlds is not like driving to the mall, Miss Barry. You will go through your training, and when you are ready, and *if* you are able to, then you will venture into that realm."

"And what do we do when we're done here?" Shan asked. "At Unit X, I mean?"

Lt. Fergie leveled a steely gaze at her and smiled. "I assure you, after you complete your training, you won't consider leaving an option. Now, if that's all, we'll continue."

Fergie did so without waiting for confirmation, and proceeded to provide a more recent overview of what Unit X was doing. The majority involved building facilities near Doors that had been discovered, which was not exciting. After that, they were handed a contract. In the end, all of them signed on, with varying degrees of consideration. Meg, Beatrice, Sil and Dave were the first to hand in their agreement. Enrique and Jonson followed shortly after.

Shan and George were left reading and rereading the contract. It was fairly straightforward, with no obvious ambiguities or doublespeak. Shan continued to delay, though she didn't know why. There was no semi-trailer to make her decision for her, she had a choice in this matter, which meant she had no choice. She closed her eyes and scrawled her name where indicated.

Upon handing it to Lt. Fergie, Shan discovered it was dinner time. The buffet featured a selection of chicken casserole and a greyish chocolate pudding. The conversation was stilted, hindered by unfamiliarity and men in suits standing silently nearby. Shan saw the guy from the gas station. He winked again. She concentrated on her pudding.

Back in the dorm, Shan fell into bed and was asleep at once. She dreamed of bloodthirsty fairies cutting her with sharp knives as she searched for a nameless child. Fergie only laughed when Shan called for help, and disappeared into a Door.

　　　***

In a matter of days, Shan no longer needed to refer to the map or have Jenkins take her to the Mess or other common spaces. A short time after that she only needed it when she was summoned to a new area.

Before the week was up, the dormitory was decorated in three different styles and far more hospitable, though it was clear Jenkins did not entirely approve. Posters covered the walls, and Meg had found a way to put her stereo system in her suitcase. Of course, that was because she came with two, and a backpack. The spare bunk was deemed the place to dump laundry, and each girl had a space on the counter in the bathroom for personal items.

On Mondays and Thursdays, the Communications Center was open to the recruits for an hour after dinner. They could use the computer and the phones. There was no cell reception but there was a landline, with an old-fashioned rotary phone. Shan called her friends, not as often as she should, but enough to let them know she was still alive. They seemed happy to know she was doing okay, even if she still hadn't "found herself."

The first real class Shan had was a rather dry history of Unit X and Fairy given in narrated slide-shows and short video clips, elaborating on Mr. Sanders being captured and tortured by fairies and escaping back to this world to form Unit X and save the world. Names and dates began blurring into each other. Only George and the kid in the Tolkien shirt seemed fascinated.

The next week flew by in a blur of tests, pre-exams and exams. Most of these made no sense, and Shan found it easiest to go on gut instinct than try to think them through. She didn't know how she did, but she wasn't kicked out of Unit X so she figured she must have passed with some degree of acceptability.

Then they embarked upon the real training. There were too many professors and instructors to remember, but it became less confusing as the training progressed and the teachers became regular and recognized. Shan was frequently struck by the similarity to her classes at County Kirk Community College, though in the beginning the most memorable thing about these classes were the several people in dark suits and darker glasses that were present at all times, taking notes or just watching. Shan was sure more lurked behind hidden panels or one-way glass. Somehow the guy from the gas station always managed to be visible in her classes.

Fairy Magic 101 and 201 was followed by Spell Classification 101. Mixed Martial Arts was mandatory after passing a basic phys-ed course and Boot Camp. After attempting a set of push-ups, Shan figured she would probably die in hand to hand combat. In their second week the recruits were assigned permanent partners.

"A buddy system," Beatrice said with a relieved smile.

There was no particularly obvious rhyme or reason to the partnerships. Neither brains nor brawn was an indication, nor comparative performance. They argued about it over meals for three days, until Jonson spoke up in a rare moment of loquaciousness.

"It is most likely they have a complex algorithm to determine the greatest compatibility based on a large correlation of data-points indexing aptitude, personality, intelligence and potential," the little oriental boy said.

"Like a dating website," Sil said, and that was the end of that.

Dave the linebacker was paired with Beatrice. Enrique and Jonson were put together, as were Sil and Meg. Meg tried to get Beatrice to agree to a switch, to no avail. Shan was not disappointed with her partner. George topped all the classes and assignments, and though he could not compare with Dave in the physical arena, Shan figured George would be the only reason she survived an encounter with the Fairies.

That inevitable event plagued her dreams and whenever

she was diagramming the proper sequence for taking out fairy mages in Ambush and Battle Tactics 101A. She hoped she didn't screw up too badly and really end up dying. That was not going to forward her plans at all. Shan continued to cling tight to the idea that the training would prepare her, and that everything would be alright.

Finally, after a month and a half, they got their first glimpse of what they had all been waiting for. The schedule introduced it as Fairy Magic 401 and directed them to a small corner of the second level. They were seated in a circle in one of the more comfortable classrooms Shan had been in, a cozy octagon with old-fashioned chairs and short bookshelves with real books on them. There were no windows, but the walls were painted with scenes of the outdoors.

The Instructor was Mr. Parke, a handsome, middle-aged man with salt-and-ginger hair. He wore no rank insignia on his plain clothes, but something about him spoke of rank in louder volumes than a hundred medals and a mile of gold braid.

"Would you like to learn about Doors?" Mr. Parke began with a teasing smile. "You're all familiar with them, I trust?"

"When one closes another one opens," Meg said.

Noting the expression Mr. Parke threw her way, Meg found her fingernails intensely fascinating.

"I'm pretty sure we were brought here using Doors," George spoke up.

"Mr. McCartney is correct," Mr. Parke nodded. "Doors. They take many forms. The most common and by far the simplest is a literal door, as you have seen, but they can be many other things. Large cracks or gaps between two objects, mirrors, and cupboards are some examples. I have even found a shadow at a particular time of day became a Door. Doors are very sophisticated magic, and..."

"Wait a moment. I thought no human had enough Fairy in them to work magic?" George interrupted.

"Though all with fairy blood have an aptitude for magic, only one in one hundred million can work any sort of *real* magic," Mr. Parke agreed.

"That's less than a hundred," Jonson said after a moment.

"Seventy-two, to be precise," Mr. Parke said. "That we know of."

"Are you one of them?" Meg asked.

Mr. Parke winked. "I'll leave that to your best guess. Mr. McCartney, I assume your question was leading to a point?"

"Well, if we can't use magic, then why do we have to learn about Doors?"

"Good question. Humans can't *make* them, but we can find them, open and close them. Possibly we can destroy them. Unit X is all about Doors. There is a unit working on a map showing all access points between this world and Fairy. The more complete the map, the easier it is to defend incursions from Fairy."

"But, if they wanted to take over the world, why don't they just make a big Door and attack?" Dave asked.

"The first thing one must understand about magic is that there are rules. Magic is as different from physics as light is to shadow, but the rules are just as precise and invariable. You have one world and you have a different and distinct world." Mr. Parke held his hands slightly apart to illustrate. "If you open a tiny crack, nothing much will change. However, if you were to widen the crack and widen the crack, eventually it would destabilize the worlds and they would collapse into each other. Everything would go *boom!* and that would be the end of that. Does that answer your question Mr. Rogers?"

Dave nodded slowly and Mr. Parke smiled.

"Good. Now, for a little demonstration of what your training will hopefully culminate in." He lowered his voice ominously. "There is a Door in this very room. Who can find it?"

Shan looked around the room, but it took George less than three seconds to point to the wall that depicted a young girl, She was looking out of the arched entrance of a gazebo to a vineyard that spread to misty foothills in the distance.

"Very good." Mr. Parke sounded as though he may be trying to hide surprise. "Now, who would like to open it? No, not you Mr. McCartney. How about quiet Mr. Chen?"

Jonson stood and walked to the wall. Examining the painting from different angles, he finally pushed against the wall, to no avail. After several attempts, he shrugged and sat down.

The others tried to the same result, even George, who took his failure personally.

"Well, all in good time," Mr. Parke said.

He opened it without even glancing at it, and the picture moved subtly, giving the impression of vast space behind it. A cool breeze blew past their faces. "Would you like a look?"

The group surged up to see. Shan peeked through and saw a world that positively glistened with magic. It was in the trees and the blue sky, the vague outline of a fortress on a rise in the distance, and the purple peaks of mountains beyond that. It was so stunning, for a moment she forgot who she was and why she was there.

They left Mr. Parke's class full of fire and purpose. The brief taste of Fairy had heated their blood and that class quickly became the favorite. However, only George began having private lessons with Mr. Parke. They began claiming more and more of his time, and other classes were dropped. Shan found herself assigned as a third wheel in one of the other partnerships more and more often.

Even when he did show up, George was preoccupied and distant. At mealtimes he no longer joined in any of the conversation and banter. The others brushed it off as a side-effect of an intense schedule and overload of homework, but Shan didn't buy that.

Shan tried to quash her growing resentment at his inattention, to tell herself that she was more than smart enough and didn't need a partner to succeed in her training. In any event, she was only staying to bring back her child.

***

As the weeks progressed, the material began to get more serious and deadly. After showing them how to open and close Doors, Mr. Parke showed them how a Door could be made into a deathtrap, sucking one into a nightmare of epic design. After Marital Arts they graduated to Weapons Training. As guns were of no use against fairies, they were given a dagger to accustom them to carrying a weapon.

The Weapons Master, Major Trimly, a short, bulldog of a man, never smiled and made it perfectly clear he thought they had absolutely no chance of survival if they came up against the Fairies in any sort of combat. He stood in front of the class, hands clasped behind his back, gruff voice barking information like a machine gun.

"These are made of silver-kissed iron. Our human heritage gives us immunity. It's deadly to fairies. One cut disables their ability to recharge magic. Iron is your best friend, make no mistake. It's kill or be killed. Expect no mercy, and give no quarter."

Shan looked down at the stiletto. It felt unnatural in her hand, and her fingers burned with the unpleasant tingle she had come to recognize as a sign of magic. Pulling the sleeve of her jumpsuit over her hand helped a little.

"Cool," Dave said with a broad grin, feinting jabs and slashes.

George frowned at his weapon, chewing on his bottom lip. When the bell signaled the end of class, he bolted. He wasn't at dinner or Diplomatic Rights and Regulations 201. Shan tried to concentrate on what she was supposed to do if she was captured and interrogated by trolls as opposed to goblins, but her thoughts kept slipping. After two hours of memorizing dates of treaties and paragraphs from the POW handbook, free period started. It was supposed to be for catching up on study, but for the girls it was mani/pedi/spa time.

Shan hurried behind Meg and Beatrice as they made their way to the dormitory, their animated chatter white noise to her. As she turned the corner, she bumped into someone, and looked up. The apology died on her lips when she saw the professor.

Mr. Parke smiled at her, a preoccupied expression lingering on his face. "Oh, Ms. Barry. How are you today?"

"Fine, thank you, Mr. Parke. Are you alright?"

"Yes, thank you. Just a few too many balls in the air and fires that need putting out at one time. It happens here on occasion. Have you seen George, by chance?"

"No, sir," Shan said. "Not since this morning."

"Ah. Well, if you do, please tell him I'd like to see him right away."

"Yes, sir." Shan was confused. "But doesn't he have

lessons with you after lunch?"

"Yes he does," Mr. Parke said. "But he has been forgetting that more often of late. Good evening, Ms. Barry."

Shan watched the retreating back of the professor, and tried not to let the thought that something was very wrong take root in her mind. She ran to catch up to Meg and Beatrice. While the other girls painted their nails and put clay face masks on, Shan paced the small room, wondering what she should do.

"What are you getting all worked up about?" Meg asked, as she put on a second coat of bright purple nail polish on her toes.

"George," Shan said, absentmindedly. "I don't know where he is."

"Oooo," Meg squealed. "Do you like him?"

"Hmmm?" Shan said. "What? No?!"

Meg raised an eyebrow in disbelief.

"Mr. Parke wanted to see him," Shan said. "I'm going to go find him."

"Try the Library," Beatrice suggested. "I've often seen him head down that way after meals."

"You mean he's been ditching me *and* Mr. Parke for the *Library*?" Shan said.

"Sil tells me George leaves in the middle of the night to have clandestine meetings with high-ranking officials. I think he's making it up, but you never know," Meg said, and a smile grew on her face. "Are you sure there's not something more to this?"

"I think there is, but not what you're thinking," Shan said. "I'll be back."

***

The basement had the feel of a Roman torture chamber. Huge columns supported the arched ceiling and rows upon rows of shelves held books of all shapes and sizes. Egyptian stone tablets, ancient scrolls, medieval tomes, rice paper covered in oriental characters, slim dime novels, college textbooks and paperbacks crammed the shelves, all containing information about Fairy, even if it was only a single paragraph or one line.

Most of the Library was dark, which highlighted the

yellow glow of lantern light in one corner. Shan walked towards it at a slow, easy pace, rehearsing her speech and trying to make it sound less accusatory or interrogatory.

Right in the middle of the bit where she explained that there must be a good reason they were made partners, she rounded a bookshelf and saw him at the other end, his back to her. He was surrounded by a glittering blue glow and floating in midair.

Her gasp echoed through the vast hall. George turned and looked down. Catching sight of her, surprise flickered across his face and he fell toward the floor with a panicked yell. Grabbing a shelf to slow his fall only resulted in a pile of books cascading after him, burying him in yellowed pages and dusty covers.

Shan turned and ran.

Footsteps followed her. She ran harder but still George, or whatever he *really* was, gained on her. Fingers brushed at her elbow and she spun, drawing her dagger and brandishing it as menacingly as possible, trying to remember what Major Trimly had taught them.

"Stay away from me!" she warned as George approached, his hands held out.

"Shan," he said. "I can explain everything."

Shan suppressed a hysterical laugh. "Really? You can explain floating in midair? I would love to hear that."

George gave her a pained look. "It's not what you think."

"I have enough soap opera clichés in my life. Spare me. What are you?"

"I'm George McCartney. I'm just who I've always said I was."

Shan pursed her lips, the dagger still pointed squarely at his chest. He didn't move, waiting to see what she would do. After a very long minute, Shad admitted to herself that she couldn't stand there forever and she wasn't up to being able to kill him. George smiled when her arm went down.

"Let me just pack up and I'll tell you everything."

Shan watched him as he went back to the books that had fallen from their shelves and began to stack them neatly together. With only the slightest hint of trepidation he reshelved them with the aid of his newfound levitation ability. He grabbed his bag and coat, and beckoned Shan forward.

"Come on. I've got something to show you."

***

They walked through passages and down stairways Shan would bet weren't on any maps of the complex. If they were, they were definitely marked with red bars. George wouldn't say anything and put a finger to his lips when she opened her mouth to start plying him with questions. As they descended a stairway darker and danker than all the others, he took her hand and helped her over the broken and protruding stones.

"Where are we going?" she growled though she did not refuse his offer of aid.

"A place where they won't be able to track or spy on us, even if they have bugged you and your stuff."

"What?" she asked. "They wouldn't..."

"Sure," he said, deadpan. "I mean, a secret agency with secrets?" Then his eyes brightened and his mouth curved up in a mischievous grin. "But wait till you see this!"

A tingle of magic running over her skin told Shan they had passed through a barrier of some sort. Her surroundings changed from a dank passageway to a landing at the bottom of a stairway. The stairway led to a small round chamber. White marble walls glowed with an inner light and tiny golden motes drifted through the air. A carpet of red velvet worn almost through in most places covered the floor. A leafless tree grew from a hole in the middle of the floor. Silver bark reflected a multitude of colors, colors Shan couldn't be sure of the source of. The whole place made her blood spark and her breath quicken.

"Isn't it magical?" George breathed as he took an enthralled circuit of the room.

"Yes," Shan said. "And that's a problem. What have you gotten yourself into, levitating and...whatever else you're doing?"

George shook his head. "We've been misled."

"Just...start from the beginning," Shan said, sitting among the roots of the tree.

Somewhere wind-chimes tinkled soothingly. George sat beside her, comfortably cross-legged. Shan couldn't remember seeing him so relaxed, and she calmed down just a little.

"It started shortly after Mr. Parke showed us how to open Doors. I found this journal in the Library," he said, his eyes lighting up. "It belonged to a recruit from about fifty years ago. Mark Jensen. It was quite fascinating - gave an interesting perspective on the events of that time."

"And?" Shan asked.

"*And*...it said that he was working for the fairies..."

"A double agent?" Shan gasped.

George nodded. "There's more. He explained how he was contacted by a fairy and given the other side of the story. *Their* side of the story. *Our* side of the story. And I found a Door, quite by accident or so I thought, *in the book.*"

Shan stared at him, sure he had gone mad. The expression on his face put uncomfortable thoughts in her head. When he saw she understood, a slow smile spread across his face and he nodded.

"You didn't?" Shan's eyes darted to the shadows of the room, trying to pick out the monsters she now suspected were lurking there. "George! What were you thinking?"

"I was thinking that it's possible those running Unit X lied to us." He rolled his eyes and gave an impatient huff when Shan's horror did not fade. "Don't you find it odd that in all our training we've never seen a real fairy, alive or dead?"

"We're not ready yet," Shan said in a small voice.

"Shan, people believe things others tell them, convinced of the absolute and unshakable infallibility of men, when ten thousand years of their own history prove without doubt that they are anything but. I took a leap of faith and contacted the Fairies."

Shan felt like crying. This was not how this was supposed to go. "I have to tell Fergie."

George wasn't fazed. "Don't be so jejune," he said.

She blinked, wondering if he was spell casting in Fairy.

"That means childish. It's French."

"I'm not being childish, or...or whatever," she snapped.

"I know it sounds a little..."

"Far-fetched?" she supplied. *What did that mean about the*

photo they had given her?

"Twisting the truth to suit certain ends can have an insidious effect on your thinking process," he countered. "For arguments sake, what if the fairies are right?"

Shan didn't know what to think about that. George looked like he came to some decision. Shan figured she wasn't going to like it. She was right.

"Next week, I'm taking you to meet Daeras."

"Who?"

"The Faerie liaison."

***

Even after a week, Shan had not come to terms with what George had told her. It threw everything into question, and opened up unpleasant possibilities. She tried not to think of that as she waited nervously at their rendezvous point outside the library. The entirety of Saturday was a free period. It was the perfect time to slip away unnoticed. Shan hadn't told anyone where she was going. She hadn't wanted to give Meg more fuel for her erroneous suspicions about Shan and George.

A moment later George came running down the hall. For a moment, Shan was alarmed, but his smile reassured her.

"Ready?" George asked.

"I'm here, aren't I? And I'm only here to *listen*." Shan's noncommittal answer didn't dampen George's spirits.

"How far is it?" Shan asked as they started walking down the hall.

"Not far," he said with a mysterious smile.

He wasn't lying. Around the next bend was another nondescript stone hallway. At the far end it was pitch dark. George took a few steps then stopped. He stood there, doing nothing while Shan became increasingly agitated.

"Well?" Shan finally blurted.

George turned to her and smiled. "Soon. Ah. Here we are."

A door had appeared in the wall. It was so different yet so familiar the hair stood up on Shan's arms.

"Real magic," George leaned close and whispered. "Let's go."

He opened the door and held it ready for her. Shan

stepped through, the tingle of magic dancing across her skin different somehow, stronger yes, but more intricate and far older than anything she had experienced. She stepped out into the back corner of the library. A perfect circle was lit with the beautiful glow of moonlight. Everything else was swallowed in darkness.

"What..." Shan began but another voice cut her off.

"George! What is the meaning of this?"

"It's okay, she's fine." George stepped in front of Shan.

Getting the distinct impression George was being protective, she peeked around him and gaped. A creature, mostly humanoid, stood next to the shelves. It came up to George's chest and had beautiful wings of lavender and white. Wild hair flamed around his face. His clothes were silk and rose petal, he wore no shoes and a variety of weapons belted to various limbs.

"*She* is the new development?" the fairy said.

"Yes," George said. "She saw me flying in the library, and I didn't see another option."

"What is your name?" the fairy asked Shan, his voice compelling her to answer.

"My name is Shanaye Amelia Barry," she said. Responding less formally felt wrong.

The fairy started. "That's...oddly reassuring."

"It is?"

"Your name - Shanaye - it means *beautiful one from a fairy place.*"

"Oh," Shan smiled. "That's pretty."

"You never told me what my name means," George said, put out.

"That's because it means *tiller of the soil,*" the fairy said. "And it wasn't important because I arranged *your* coming."

"Oh." George looked apologetic. "Sorry. This was the best I could manage on short notice."

"Don't do it again," Daeras said, evidently accepting the apology. "Too much is at stake."

The dream Shan kept trying to wake herself from was becoming increasingly real, and she was having difficulty remembering how to breath.

"I need to sit down."

The fairy waved his hand and a chair appeared. Actually, it was a toadstool with a very comfortable moss cushion, but Shan's knees gave out before she had time to register that.

"Okay, so what is going on?" she said.

"You didn't tell her?" Daeras said, a frown flashing across his smooth face.

"I gave her a brief overview," George hedged. "She was in a small state of shock at the time, so I don't know how much she retained..."

"I'm right here," Shan said, glaring up at him. "And I *retained* everything you said. About the journal. And other stuff."

"Maybe you should start at the beginning," George told Daeras.

"Very well," the fairy sighed.

He settled himself several inches above the floor, crossing his legs and folding his wings back. A glittering blue aura surrounded him and Shan understood where George had learned that trick, though she still couldn't believe it was possible. *Could George be the one-in-a-hundred-million?*

The fairy cleared his throat and began to speak.

"The political geography between Fairy and the Mortal Realm is colorful and turbulent. Our Historians put our first interaction thousands of years ago, at the end of your Greco-Roman times, when the Fairies brought the Druids their seventh gift. It was at that same time the indiscretions that resulted in humans with Fairy blood were most common.

"Before the Great War in which the Barriers to keep men out were erected, men and fairy often visited each other's lands. In your year 1752, one such guest in Fairy was called Herman Sanders. He attempted to steal the King's Crown and was imprisoned. While in prison, he poisoned the mind of a particular fairy called Nabil, the Outcast. The son of the king, Nabil wished to have the throne for himself. For if he had the throne, he would have the crown. The Crown is the key to magic. It allows a person to tap into the seams of magic that bind Fairy together. In the wrong hands, it would wreak havoc.

"But the king chose Nabil's brother to rule instead.

Herman Sanders promised he could get the crown for Nabil, if he was freed. Herman Sanders murdered the king and his heir, and went for the crown. But Fate intervened. Before he could take the crown, Estrada, daughter of the Court's High Mage took up the fallen King's sword, and Herman Spencer and Nabil were forced to flee through the King's own Door into this world. Fairy put wards to keep them out, and they've been trying to get back ever since."

"For three hundred years?" Shan asked.

"Magic," George said. "It does funny things with time."

"Sanders is long dead, but Nabil is still out there," Daeras said. "He is the true force behind Unit X, though he can only accomplish his goal using the talents of men with fairy blood."

"That's what Fergie said," Shan said.

"One of the truths that holds Unit X together." The fairy shook his head. "Something built entirely of lies will fall apart. A sprinkling of truth prolongs its life."

"What about...what about my son? Is that true?" Shan said, the crux of the problem lying on the fairy's answer.

If George was surprised about her revelation, he didn't show it. Daeras only looked confused. "I don't know what you mean."

"Unit X said the Fairies had kidnapped my son because he was like me," Shan said. "They would use him to get into our world."

Daeras stepped up to her and extended his hand. "May I?"

Shan nodded. Daeras pressed his fingers to her forehead. With a white flash, the picture came to mind, of her son and the fairy. Daeras gasped and pulled away, his face twisted.

"That child is in danger, but not from who you think," he said. "The creature beside him, that is Nabil."

"But he has no wings," Shan said.

"He forsake his wings when he left," Daeras said, the bite in his tone only slightly less frightening than his expression.

Shan frowned. Her gut told her the fairy was not lying. But that meant that the past weeks she had been aiding the monsters who took her son. But maybe not...if she used the things she had learned against Unit X, perhaps she could still get him back.

"Just help us keep it hidden," the fairy asked. "If those running Unit X ever find a way into Fairy, war will be unavoidable. If we maintain the barriers, keep Fairy hidden, bloodshed untold will be averted."

"What about my son?"

"He is somewhere in this world. Perhaps somewhere in this very building," Daeras said.

A growl and an earsplitting shriek reverberated from behind them.

***

Daeras bolted straight up, a golden sword drawn. George and Shan stood as well, ears and eyes straining into the gloom. Inarticulate whimpers came closer. A human voice spoke, the syllables desperate. Another growl came, softer this time, the warning clear. A shape stepped into the light and Daeras put away his sword.

The creature was huge, two and a half times George's height. Knobbly brown skin folded over limbs as thick as tree branches, the proportions of its face were almost comical, no ears, small eyes, large nose, larger mouth. It held Meg by one leg. Her face was pale, making her red hair even redder, and tears had dragged mascara across her face.

"Urlung, put her down. Now."

The creature made a face, pulling the already incongruous features further out of alignment. It muttered something, a long grumble ending in a whine.

"I know. But not here. And speak in English so our new friends can understand, please."

"Friends do not spy on each other," Urlung said, his speech only slightly more comprehensible.

"I wasn't spying..." Meg said.

"Friends do not lie either," Urlung growled and gave Meg a shake.

"Urlung!" Daeras snapped.

The creature shrugged and set Meg down, not gently but he did refrain from dropping her.

"Who is this?" Daeras asked.

"Meg," Shan said, helping her friend to her feet. "Meg, what are you doing here?"

"I was only trying to see if you and George were, you know..." Meg said, and raised an eyebrow. "So, what's up? Who's the ogre? And the short guy?"

"The ogre is a *troll* and his name is Urlung," Urlung said. "He is bodyguard to the short guy."

"And the short guy is Daeras," George said. "He's the First Captain of the Kingsguard and my liaison to the Fairy."

"You're taking this pretty calmly," Shan said, glancing at Meg. "It took me at least..."

"At least a week to process it?" Meg said and smirked. "That's because you think too much. It's a fairy. Here. In the school. And you're talking to it. It hasn't killed you. Everything's okay. End of story."

"And that's cool with you?" Shan said.

"Yup. Pretty much." Meg wiped her face and gave her hair a finger-comb before hooking her thumbs in the belt of her jeans. "And now that I'm here, somebody want to explain what we're going to do?"

"What do you mean, what *we're* going to do?" George said.

"Yeah. I heard everything. Bad people want to murder the Fairy King and steal the Crown. We have to do something about that."

George groaned. "No. You don't get it. We can't let them know we know. It will ruin everything."

"So, we'll be like a...a..."

"A cabal."

Meg blinked rapidly. Shan didn't bother asking.

George shrugged. "It's a secret political faction."

"Okay, you have *got* to stop reading the Thesaurus," Meg said. "Great. We're a cabal. What does that mean we *do*?"

George put his hands on his hips and cast his eyes upward. "We aren't going to *do* anything. We mustn't do anything to make them suspect."

"The Fairies are working on *truly* sealing up the Doors permanently, as Unit X purportedly does," Daeras said. "It takes time. Our grandfathers had a twisted sense of humor and many of them were more powerful than we are now. When you find the Doors, you must send word to us via the journal and we will make closing those doors a priority."

"Can we tell the others?" Meg asked.

"No!" George said sharply. "We can take no chances. You weren't even supposed to be here."

Meg rolled her eyes. "Don't get your knickers in a knot, smarty. I'm not stupid. I won't tell anyone."

George looked mollified but not convinced. Daeras was less so.

"You two must swear a Blood Oath," the Fairy said, staring at Shan and Meg.

"Sounds pleasant," Meg said. "What for?"

"It will assure your cooperation and your silence with magic and blood, binding your immortal soul to your word," Urlung said, his lips pulling up in something between a grin and a snarl. "And if you attempt to break it, it will cause a very painful and prolonged death."

Meg looked troubled for less than a second, then she nodded. "Cool."

"Meg, you're insane," Shan said, shaking her head.

It was not something to take lightly, what this fairy was demanding. Magic was not something to be trifled with, and certainly not when it had to do with blood and one's word on their immortal soul.

"Out of curiosity, what will you do if we refuse?" Shan asked, no surer of this than she had been about Unit X.

"You have done nothing to harm us and do not deserve to be imprisoned or executed. We will magically wipe your memory," Daeras explained as though he were listing the lunch specials. "You will remember nothing and will be no threat to us. It will not be painful and you will not be further violated."

"If we work for Unit X, doesn't that constitute a threat?" Meg said, more sarcastically than Shan thought was prudent.

"We're trying not to get ourselves killed here Meg," Shan said. "How can you be so sure we won't remember? There are always ways to bring back memories."

Urlung snorted and a haughty expression crossed

Daeras's face. "Perhaps with your crude *scientific* methods," he said. "Not so with magic. Magic is pure. Everything that can be done with your methods can be done better with magic." He snapped his fingers. "You recall the Space-Time Warp Unit X used to contact you?"

Shan nodded. Daeras looked triumphant.

"Scientifically impossible. But with magic...!" he waved his hand, as if that explained everything.

"Wait, someone in Unit X can use magic?" Meg said with a frown.

"Apparently," George said, with a significant glance at Daeras.

"So we have to ferret him out as well?" Meg said. "Or her?"

"No," George said. "We must do nothing, *nothing*, to call attention to ourselves. At all."

Meg nodded solemnly. "Nothing at all. Got it."

Shan resisted the urge to say something about floating in the Library and instead looked at Daeras. "So, about this Blood Oath?"

***

"It's not complicated," Daeras said.

"I've already gone through it," George said. "And I'm still alive."

The joke didn't get a response. George sighed. "So did you bring the stuff you need?"

Daeras nodded. Shan frowned.

"I wanted him to be prepared," George said. "You know, in case you decided to, um, join the resistance."

"That is so Star Wars," Shan said.

"Awesome. I'm in," Meg said.

Shan nodded.

Daeras pulled out a small golden flask from somewhere in the air and gave it a vigorous shake. Then he drew a golden knife with five pale blue stones arranged in an arch on the hilt.

"You're both going to drink this, then draw blood on your palms. Hold my hand and repeat the words I say."

Shan and Meg glanced at each other and then held out

their hands. Daeras handed the flask first to Shan. The liquid was as thick as honey, sweet and slightly tangy, with flavors of orange and mint overlaying jasmine and vanilla. It was effervescent and her nose tingled. She and Meg swallowed, and pricked their hands. Then Daeras took the knife and cut both his hands. His grip was firm when he took theirs.

"Drem tae urd long Fairy emne..." he paused. The silence stretched longer. "Repeat it aloud."

Shan knew what the words meant. *I swear to keep the secret of the Fairy...* "Drem tae urd long Fairy emne..."

"Drem tae urd long Fairy emne..." Meg said.

George mouthed the words along with them.

"Dris eft nordor tem, cas tae, cas men ay..." *Outside the knowledge of* (some phrase translating to *outsider* or *one in the shadows*), *in darkness, in silence.*

"Dris eft nordor tem, cas tae, cas men ay..." Shan and Meg chorused.

"Ester em doom."

"Ester em doom." *Forever until death.*

A tingle of magic ran through Shan, intensifying until it felt like her skin was going up in flames. Then it disappeared in a gust of icy air, leaving her gasping.

"Whew!" Meg said. "That was a rush!"

"Do you need a Band-Aid?" George asked Shan, gesturing to her hand.

"No, it was just a nick," Shan said.

"I'd love a Band-Aid, thanks George," Meg said, batting her eyelids at him.

George rolled his eyes. Daeras put away his knife and the flask, a satisfied expression on his timeless and youthful face. "It is done."

"So what do we do *now*?" Meg asked for the umpteenth time.

Find my son, Shan thought, looking down at the cut on her hand. Wherever that takes me.

Looking up, she caught Meg's eyes, then George's. They looked determined, and their expressions gave Shan some hope and comfort. They had different reasons, but they were in on this together now. Daeras drew them in close, his lavender wings fluttering.

"You will continue as you have. Help us keep Fairy safe. And one day, we may hope, Unit X will quietly close its doors, and Fairy will know peace."

About Nicole DragonBeck

Nicole was born in California one snowy summer long ago, the illegitimate offspring of an elf and a troll. At a young age her powers exploded and she was banished to the wilderness of South Africa because her spells kept going inexplicably awry. There she was raised by a tribe of pygmy Dragons and had tremendous adventures, including defeating a terrible Fire-Demon that had been tormenting a sect of Dwarf priests. In gratitude they taught her the arcane magic of writing and the rest is horribly misinterpreted history. She reads as much as she writes, is obsessed with dragons and Italians, enjoys cooking, listening to music and can often be heard fiddling on a keyboard or guitar. She currently lives in Clearwater, Florida, is a member of The Ink Slingers Guild and is working on several novels, all of which have at least one mention of a dragon. She lists friends, music and life among her greatest influences.

Connect with Nicole online:
nicoledragonbeck.com
facebook.com/nicolebeckauthor
twitter.com/DragonBeck

Other books by Nicole DragonBeck
First Magyc (Book One in the Guardians of the Path series)
On the Verge (Anthology)
Behind the Veil (Anthology)
The Death of Jimmy (Anthology)
Into the Abyss (Anthology)
Beyond the Threshold (Anthology)

Bump in the Night

By Dee Rea

Crouched down behind an old Ford 150, clutching a kitchen knife in my shaking hand, all I could think about was the last thing my sister said to me.

Every muscle in my body was taut and my breath caught in my throat when an empty soda can rattled across the pavement beside the truck. I was afraid to look. Instead, I did a sort of backwards shimmy under the truck as I tried to hide myself a little better. I wasn't sure what had kicked that can and I wasn't about to be surprised by it either. I quickly realized I was still pretty much out in the open, but it was better than nothing. Once fully underneath, I tried to see what had set the lovely little tin can alarm off. In the fray, I'd lost sight of my mom and dad, as well as my brothers and sister. I hoped that I would see a familiar set of shoes. I saw nothing.

Exhaling a long slow breath to calm myself, I folded my arms on the ground and rested my chin on them. Every sense was heightened from the adrenaline that raced through my veins. I needed to take a moment to digest the past month and a half, if only to calm my rattled nerves. It all seemed surreal, like something I'd seen in a movie or three. Everything had happened so quickly, and yet it felt like everything had taken an eternity. Was that even possible? I couldn't help but wonder if news reports in other places truly showed the extent of the horrors or if they sugarcoated it like they had here.

The nightmare of an adventure began when my parents had the wonderful idea to go on a vacation. The concept of a vacation in my parents' minds was stuffing the entire family into an RV and driving to see our grandmother who lived across the country. I thought it was really strange because we'd never taken a real vacation. Our vacations consisted of trips to the zoo on discount days. We weren't exactly poor, but some weeks existing was more of a struggle than others. We'd been on the road taking in all the usual tourist traps for about two weeks when my parents disclosed a little secret they'd neglected to share previously. They felt a truck stop eatery was the perfect place to tell my older sister and myself.

"Sebastian, stop playing with your food. You love applesauce!" Mom said with an exaggerated sigh. Getting the twins to eat was always a chore.

"Mommy, it's not cold! I don't like warm applesauce!" Jonathan cried in dismay. He was the voice of the twins. Sebastian rarely spoke, he didn't have to.

"Jonny listen to your mother. Sebastian, at least eat your macaroni. You both love that, warm or cold for reasons that escape me," Dad said sternly, yet not harshly. He had a knack of chastising us without ever raising his voice that made us feel horribly guilty.

"Potty, Daddy," Sebastian said in his usual quiet manner.

"Don't worry, Dad, I'll take them," Ricky said as he put his fork down.

"Thank you, son," Mom said, rubbing her temples. When the three brothers got lost in the hustle of the restaurant, she looked at dad and nodded.

"Girls, your mother and I have to tell you something. We're not just going to see Memaw for fun or a vacation..." Dad started. We were driving out to our grandmother's house to settle some random uncle's will. Apparently, my parents had failed to mention that our uncle was one of those dotcom ridiculously rich types. This uncle, whom I'd never met, was apparently the black sheep of the family because he was gay or something old-fashioned like that. The rest of the family had followed my Grandfather's wishes and disassociated themselves from him. Everyone, that is, except my mom. She told us that was why she had been named the sole heir to his estate.

"So you mean we're loaded now?" Olivia asked and I giggled at her blunt manner. She wasn't known for her tact.

"In a manner of speaking, yes we are. Your father and I have both taken extended time off of work to drive out there. We could have flown, but we were uncomfortable with leaving you kids at home alone. I'm sure you're well aware the neighborhood isn't what it used to be." Mom looked at dad with the same tired worried look I'd seen so many times before.

"Mom, it's not like it's the murder capital of the world. I've never even seen a crow!" Olivia laughed at her own wittiness.

"Olivia, don't be such a cunning linguist! You know we've never seen more than a clowder!" I couldn't help myself.

"Girls!" Our father gave us a stern look and we both looked down at the table.

"Sorry Papa," I muttered. I lifted my gaze and watched my brothers reappear. The rest of the meal was more subdued. I watched as the red-faced waitress raced from the manager over to cut the TV off. Apparently the manager didn't want to watch the news when the headline read 'Another unexplained murder'. I shrugged it off. Who wanted to watch blood or murder when they were eating? I knew I didn't. I chewed on the back of my lip ring as I thought about what my parents had told my sister and I. It was hard to digest the fact that we were now rich. I wouldn't have to watch my parents struggle and work so hard. It had to be a good thing right?

A week after their little revelation and much sight-seeing later, we'd broken down in a little shithole of a town somewhere in New Mexico. I suppose there's a 'wrong turn in Albuquerque' joke in there somewhere but right now, it's lost on me. I don't know for sure what even broke. I just know we were cruising along, watching the sun lowering to kiss the horizon, when there was a loud pop and steam roared from the engine, fogging the outside of the window.

"I'll call a tow truck. The attorney did say that all we had to do was give him the receipts from the credit card and our trip would be on him per Georgie's instructions," Mom said with a grin.

"I don't know how he did that, but bless him for being a smooth talker I guess," Dad laughed. We all watched as mom called a local tow truck company. I was glad I'd taught her how to use her phone to search for things near wherever you are. I could just see her getting a towing company from back home in the 'Burg. The younger siblings were inside still playing their card game. They'd been playing it for hours. It was based on some anime and the rules didn't make much sense to me but it kept them occupied.

"How long until it gets dark?" Olivia asked, squinting in the sun's direction. "I read somewhere that it gets cold in the desert even when it's roasting hot during the day."

"We have an hour or an hour and a half I'd say," Dad said as he walked over to put his arm around his eldest daughter's shoulders. "We won't freeze because we'll be in a motel. It may even have a pool. It may even have Wi-Fi."

"Oh! All is right in the world, if the motel has internet!" Olivia quipped. We all loved her sense of humor. Some would say she had a dry and sarcastic sense of humor and others would just say she was a snob. We loved her for it.

"Don't worry, Livy. We'll be ok," Dad whispered. Had I not been right beside them, I wouldn't have heard him. I hoped he was right. We watched the lights of the tow truck glisten on the heat rising from the road. It cast an eerie orange glow to the optical illusion so that it seemed as if it was floating on water. I watched as my mother gathered the kids out of the broken RV. We stood at the grill, oblivious now to the funky smell that radiated from it.

"Mom," Ricky said as he stepped closer to the family and rested a hand on one of the twin's shoulders. "Why is the sheriff with the tow truck? We haven't..."

"Your mom told the dispatcher at the tow truck company how many of us there were and that we wouldn't all fit into the tow truck. I guess this was their solution. I wouldn't worry too much son." Our dad spoke not just to my brother, but to all of us. He beamed a smile at us each in turn and then headed over to talk to the driver. It was decided that Dad and I would ride with the tow truck driver and the rest of the family would ride with the sheriff. As soon as we got into the truck, the driver cut the radio off. On the way back, my dad bartered with the driver over the price of a rental car once he realized the driver was the company owner while I sat and wondered why any business owner would want to do the work himself.

When we reconvened at the mechanic's shop, I eyed the

motel across the street with skepticism. It looked like something out of a horror movie, the kind with a serial killer waiting for his next victim. The local sheriff strongly advised against us staying at that motel. He told us it was a haven for the less than desirable elements of life. He continued to talk to my parents in a hushed tone. I figured he was talking about junkies and criminals. Instead, he pointed us in the direction of a rather strangely outfitted hotel. The building looked like it was ready for a major hurricane, tornado and every other natural disaster all at the same time. Impervious to any and all harm, or so it seemed.

A noise on my right made me hold my breath and focus my attention back on the here and now. When I searched the darkness, I was relieved to find nothing more than the wind blowing in the distance. Okay, this is just crazy. Where was I? Oh yeah, calming myself down by reliving the past month and a half. I fought the urge to twist the piercing on my lip. I pressed my teeth together to keep my tongue from moving the stud from the inside as well. It was a bad habit that I'd had since my mom had taken me to get it done the year before. My dad had been against it, but my mother always encouraged me to express myself. She'd begrudgingly signed the permission slip at the piercing place. Nope, don't play with the sparkly stud and give away where you're hiding! No, no you don't! Back to figuring out what happened. The hotel? Yes, I was thinking about the hotel. It looked like some sort of hybrid between an A-Bomb shelter and a hurricane safe-house.

When we pulled into the hotel, it was getting close to sundown. The lady at the front desk was nice, but very firm. We had thirty minutes to get anything we wanted into the hotel before the doors locked for the night. When we began to question her, she looked at the clock and instead of answering gave us a running countdown of our time left. We took her seriously.

We quickly gathered our suitcases from the loaner car the mechanic had given us. At the exact time the clerk had said the doors would be locked, they clanked shut, and we took our stuff to the rooms.

The rooms we were given blew our minds. We'd never stayed anywhere as nice. Each room had a little kitchen area, a living room, a bedroom and a bathroom, and doors that connected the two rooms together. The way the rooms were laid out, we decided my parents would have one of the bedrooms, and Olivia and I would have the other. Each of the bedrooms had really cool pocket doors that separated them from the living rooms where the fold out couches would serve as the boys' bedrooms. The twins would stay in our parents' living room and Ricky would stay in the living room on our side.

Then we had the debate of stay in or go out and explore what areas we could. Curiosity won out in the end and we set out to explore. Dad went back to see the clerk, while Mom and I watched my siblings investigate the lobby's comforts. When Dad came back with the new info on where we could and couldn't go there was no restraining my brothers and sister. It was off to the pool. The younger ones jumped in and frolicked in the water while the parents and I found a table to sit at. That was where we met Arjun. Arjun was this really cute guy from Australia or somewhere like that. He explained that there was some sort of serial killer or pack of wild animals that only struck at night. When my mom asked about the strange acoustics of the pool area, Arjun explained that it was the hotel. He said that not only was it sealed from letting out any light sources, it was soundproofed as well.

My dad called my siblings out of the pool, deciding it was time to settle in for the night. On the way back to our prospective rooms, we saw a lady in a heated argument with the clerk. I was looking forward to a nice soft pillow so I didn't pay the scene much attention. Little did I know it was to become a nightly argument.

"Should we just leave our stuff in the suitcases or should we unpack?" Olivia asked my parents. I was glad she asked because I hadn't even thought about it. I was too busy fighting Ricky for the box of caramel coated popcorn.

"Well, we should probably at least unpack the..." My dad turned to look at Ricky and I. "Would you two please stop? I'm trying to have a conversation here!" He sighed and shook his head as he looked back to my sister. "As I was saying, we should at least unpack the essentials because we're going to be here for at least a few days, if not a week. The mechanic said that he figured it was either the radiator hose or maybe a sensor that made the RV overheat like that. If he has to order any parts we're looking at a week."

"Let's hope that it doesn't take that long," Mom said spinning as the twins ran around her playfully.

"We can unpack tomorrow. For now, I think it's time for everyone to turn in. We have a few things to do tomorrow and I want to make sure we're all up and ready early." He grinned at the chorus of 'Aww but Dads' that filled the air. I was more than ready to fall into bed. I had a hard time sleeping in the RV. It was going to be nice to sleep in a bed that didn't move and where I couldn't hear six other people breathing. I couldn't wait! I didn't even pay attention to the low mumble of the TV from my parents' room.

When my mom started cooking breakfast the next morning, I forgot for a moment where I was. I thought I was back at home and the lazy days of summer filled with hanging out with my friends, and annoying my siblings would be the bright spot of the day. When I stubbed my toe on the unfamiliar layout of the room, it all came crashing back. Soon we'd be loaded and bars on the windows would be a thing of the past. We just had to wait for the RV to get fixed before we could go see our grandmother and sign those papers.

"Morning sweetheart."

"Morning, Mom. Where are Dad and Ricky? When did you get bacon? I'm not complaining, but it smells really good."

"Dad went out as soon as the doors opened this morning. We decided to let you girls sleep. The twins were up at the crack of dawn bouncing on poor Ricky so he decided to take them down to the pool."

"After breakfast I'll go down and give Ricky a break," I said, thinking that maybe I could get an eyeful of Arjun. I was hoping so anyway. An afternoon with my younger brothers running wild wasn't my idea of a great day, but Arjun would make it worth it.

"That's really sweet of you honey, but I think your dad wants to check out a few sights around here before the RV gets fixed."

"Mom! I've had enough of the world's largest yarn balls!" I whined. I knew Dad meant well and just wanted to give us the memories that we would remember into our golden years. The thing was, I didn't care about seeing the tourist hells that we'd been seeing. They were hot and annoying, and drove all of us kids bonkers.

"Sara, just humor us okay? These are things that we've wanted to do for you kids but were never able to because we could never afford it. We're trying to take advantage of the gifts that we've been given."

"I know, I know. I get it Mom. A week at a theme park would have done the same thing and we would have had more fun there." I sighed heavily and let myself slump into a chair. "I'm sorry, Mom. I know that I'm being a shithead."

"Sara! Language!" Mom said, spinning around to face me.

"Sorry! Oh sorry sorry sorry! It's just that I feel bad for making you feel bad for trying to give us the things that you always wanted to. I know, I'm a bad kid." I rested my chin on my upturned palm and cradled my elbow on the table with my other hand. I peeked up at her sheepishly.

"You are my little rebel, but even rebels have hearts and I know you don't want to break your dear sweet parents' hearts." She winked and I knew the discussion was over. Dad and Ricky saved me from having to answer when he came in the rooms.

"If it isn't two of my most beautiful ladies!"

"Hello sweetheart, what did the mechanic say?" My mother leaned to put the plate of bacon on the table in front of me. I picked up a piece and waved at my dad as I took a bite of the crunchy deliciousness.

"Welp, it seems that we're gonna be here for a while. The mechanic wasn't there and the lady at the desk said that all of their shipments were delayed because the postman didn't show up today. I did ask if there was a different mechanic that could work on the old beater and she said that there is a part time guy, but he only comes in once a week on Saturdays. So, being that it's only Tuesday, we're here for a bit." Dad reached down to snag a piece of bacon and I growled playfully.

"A week?!?" The groan came from the doorway to the room I shared with my sister.

"Yes, a week," Dad said around a mouthful of bacon.

"What are we going to do in this rattrap of a town for a week?" Olivia huffed as she stomped over to the refrigerator. She squealed happily. "Orange juice! Oh the nectar of the gods!"
"I'm sure that there are dishes you can do, or maybe you can clean a room or two..." Mom joked.

She didn't realize how true that statement would turn out to be. We wouldn't be going anywhere because the part for the RV never came, and to make matters worse, both mechanics disappeared. We came to understand how our sanctuary continued to run efficiently. People who came to stay for any length of time, like us, became residents.

The residents pulled together to work to keep the hotel functioning in such a way as to protect us from what happened at night. There were groups, kind of like work details, that did different things like cook, clean, or go out for supplies. We, the kids, didn't think it was all that great, but being able to play for most of the day or do whatever we wanted was pretty ok payment for us. For us, the pool and endless WI-FI made up for having to do a few chores every day.

So it went, and our days turned into weeks with little notice being given. We were content and complacent in our little haven. The residents were content to wait until the powers that be came in and figured everything out. We thought we were safe and secure in our peaceful little world. Of course, we also had to deal with the crazy lady who slept all day and yelled at the night clerk about her missing son. The kid was probably worm dirt by now. Anyone that was caught outside the hotel at night was found the next morning, a pool of guts and goo. We started paying attention to the news reports that had finally started to pick up the story as the strange occurrences started happening all over. No one seemed to know what it was out in the dark, only that the bodies found in the morning were mangled and ripped apart. At least I had eye candy to keep me entertained.

"Evening Arjun! Sheriff, good to see you again," Dad said one night when we all wandered down to dinner. The twins were walking hand in hand toward the buffet, while Olivia and Ricky lagged behind watching some video online on her phone. Arjun was maybe thirty and he was really handsome. I knew he was too old for me but I could admire the view, right? I listened to the three men talk about the security of the hotel and the increase of attacks.

"He went outside weeks ago! Can't we just send a search party? I'm begging you!" The woman's shriek filled the air.

"Ma'am, we've been through this." The clerk rolled her eyes and sighed heavily. I could tell she was over having the conversation with the crazy lady. "Many times already. If you would like to request a search party, you have to do it when the hotel is open. Once the doors close, you know that we can't open them until the next morning."

"Don't bother yourself, Henry. I got her this time. Arjun, you're up next," the sheriff laughed as he went to defuse the situation with the crazy dodger who nightly harassed the poor clerk.

"Titillating isn't it? That's why geography is so important. Location, location, location." Olivia and Ricky laughed as they passed us to go sit by the pool. They'd already eaten while they helped in the kitchen. We all begrudgingly pulled our weight.

The clip clip sounds that preceded the blonde's stilettoes grated on my nerves. *Why would anyone wear shoes like that with an insidious killer lurking out in the shadows?* I thought. Hell, why would anyone wear those unless they were going to a club or trying to get attention?

"Seriously? A stiletto, now of all the shoes! Why not wear a wedge?" A newcomer asked my mother. My mom's response was a simple shrug. Mom was an angel like that. She never judged anyone for anything. We were now rich because of it, weren't we?

Oh shit! What was that? Shit shit shit! In the distance I heard an unearthly howl. Focus! Keep calm or you're going to be bloody ribbon puddles! Shit, the news. No time. Take a breath and get it together! OK, focus, the lady. The crazy lady that ended our utopia, how had she managed? She had argued with the front desk clerk for weeks before disappearing. Dad had become the unofficial leader alongside the sheriff. Dad and the guys had searched and searched for Crazy but no one ever found her. Shit, it's getting closer. Should I move? No, stay here and stay calm. Can it smell fear? Shit, I wish I'd paid attention to the news reports! Something, there is something that I need to remember about these things... Oh hell, it's close. Are those shoes? Remember! Remember what? What am I supposed to remember about these damn things?

I was sitting in the laundry, listening to the steady thump of the wet towels in the dryer. It was a soothing sound. Somehow, I got stuck on the laundry crew. I hated doing my own laundry, much less towels for a hotel full of people. Okay, so maybe it wasn't a full hotel, but when some of the locals started coming to the hotel it did seem to get a little bit crowded. There weren't that many locals to begin with. Apparently the town was a ghost of its former self. At its pinnacle, it had been home to the many families that worked for the government, the mines and whatnot. After the government stopped testing bombs in the desert, the jobs in the surrounding areas slowly dried up. The mines coughed up the last of their treasures and from what we were told it was the proverbial death blow to the baby metropolis that was trying to form. Now, it took a rare type of person to try and live here.

I was reading a book. I don't even remember what it was. Some history book because I'd always dreamt of being a historian. Maybe it was a book on the history of the town we were in. I don't remember and I don't think I cared, I just loved reading about people's lives and how they lived. I had always thought of keeping a journal so I could go back and read my own history. I never started one.

Out of the corner of my eye, I saw a shadow race across the wall at an odd angle. I snapped my head to look at the little window that led out into the hall. There was a loud clang just outside the door and my heart stopped. I stood up and slowly walked to the door. Pressing my face against the window, I searched the hallway the best way I could without opening the door. I saw a figure hunched over an overturned garbage can and smiled. It was just someone being a klutz. I could understand that, my sister said that I was the only person she knew that could trip on air. I relaxed a bit, but there was something odd about the person. Something just didn't seem right. I couldn't quite put my finger on it so I continued to watch. The form moved in a jerky and dysfunctional sort of way. I jumped when the buzzer to the dryer went off. I think I rattled the door handle, and I found out what was not right real quick. The thing, the person or whatever it was snapped upright and spun around. It was missing the majority of its guts. They weren't just hanging out. They were gone, just gone. I clamped a hand over my mouth and quickly locked the deadbolt. Backing away from the door, I yelped when I ran into the chair that I'd been sitting in. Moving around it quickly, I scanned the room for a place to hide.

There was only one door to the laundry room and I had just locked someone on the outside. Butterballs of flaming sriracha! I quickly moved to the folding table and crawled under it. Never had I been so happy to have a flimsy little curtain as I was when I pulled it shut. The rattling and thumping against the door made me jump and press both hands to my lips to keep from screaming. I heard the glass shatter and felt my heart stop. The smell instantly changed in the room. It went from a clean smell to the smell of putrid death. I closed my eyes so tight I swear I saw the universe behind my lids.

Screams shattered the silence of the night and I stared out into the darkness. My heart was beating so loudly I was sure it could be heard like a beacon. Just like the lantern in a lighthouse, yep that's my heart. It was the light that was leading all the creatures straight to me through the darkest maze. Wait a minute, what was that? Was that a car? No, it couldn't be. No one was crazy enough to drive at night! Oh sweet merciful taco shells! I blinked and tried to peer into the darkness across the parking lot to the road beyond. I was right, it had been a car. Had they made it? Would I make it? Ok, figure out what happened. Keep calm! Think, brain, think!

The monster came into the room and left. It didn't have the sense to move the curtain, luckily for me. After what felt like an eternity, the clean smell seemed to come alive again. The dryer had stopped and so had the racing of my heart, for the most part. I strained to hear any sound but all I heard was my breath. I carefully crawled out of my hiding place and gasped. The door was splintered. I eased my way toward it ready to dive back into my cubbyhole at the slightest sound. Carefully, I climbed through the remains of the door and quickly made my way over to the elevator. I pressed my hand over the buttons when the elevator announced its arrival with a ding. I felt like such an idiot! Like my hand could really dampen the sound. I jumped in and started pounding the button to the third floor. As the doors closed, the smell of death filled the elevator and I looked over in time to see a human eye in the middle of ribbons of flesh staring at me as the doors closed. I couldn't help it. I screamed.

When the elevator stopped, I didn't even wait for the doors to fully open before I sprinted down the hall toward our rooms. While I beat on the door, I turned to look over my shoulder down the hall. I knocked harder and faster when I saw the shadows along the ceiling. Why were there shadows on the ceiling?

"Mommy! Daddy! Let me in!" I screamed. I heard the locks working from the other side and still, I pounded my fists against the wood.

"Hold your horses! What's wrong with you? Everyone went down to help get ready for when we unlock," Olivia said as she stepped back rather than be bowled over by my rushing in. I quickly spun around to slam the door and fumble with the locks.

"It got in!" I shrieked. Satisfied that I had successfully managed to lock the door, I turned around and rushed over to the counter. I threw open cabinet after cabinet looking for something to calm my nerves. I knew my mom had a bottle of wine or cooking sherry, maybe even a bottle of whiskey.

"What got in, Sara? Are you crazy? Put that down! I'm not going to get into trouble for your indiscretion! No! Put down Dad's whiskey and tell me what farfetched nonsense you're babbling on about? This place is a fortress."

"Whatever is out there got in, Olivia!" I said breathlessly, trying to cling to the nefarious bottle.

"Oh Sara, stop with the jejune behavior! I told you that..."

We both turned to the door when we heard the unearthly howl.

"Sara," Olivia whispered as we reached out to cling to each other. "What was that?"

Damnation and spitballs! How many were coming toward the hotel? The howling was definitely louder. Did that mean it was closer? I looked over at the tires and wondered if I had time to climb into the cab of the truck. No, probably not. I didn't see any other option. As soon as I climb out from under the truck there was nothing around, not even a bush to hide behind. To my left was the mangled loading bay door that I assumed was how the creatures had gotten in. It seems that the crazy lady had blocked it so it wouldn't close in case her stupid son came back. Why didn't we check it? We would still be safe inside had she not been so insipid, self-centered and just plain bat-shit crazy!

"Saaarrraaaa..." The distorted voice called out and scared the daylights out of me. How did it know my name? Oh no, this can't be good. Shit! Remember, what had the news report said? Did it say how to get away? I don't remember! The only thing I can remember is the last thing my sister said to me. "Sara, did you forget to change your tampon?"

<<<<>>>>

About Dee Rea

Dee Rea is an award winning poet and author of *Journey into the Night.* She's been writing ever since she can remember, though some of her earlier works should never see the light of day. She earned her BA in Anthropology with honors and a Minor in History in 2014. She learned her love of the written word from her father. She now lives in Central Florida with her beloved family.

Connect with Dee online:
www.DeeRea.com
Twitter.com/AuthorDeeRea

Other books by Dee Rea
Journey into the Night

The River

By JM Paquette

"Remind me why we are doing this again?" Hannah asked, hunkering on one knee and rubbing her barked shin. She glared at the responsible rock, then transferred the glare to her husband.

The elf stared down at her, face impassive. "Is it bad?" Rory jerked his head at her shin.

Hannah wiped the blood away and flipped her dress down, hiding the scrape from his view as she got to her feet. She stared at the blood smeared on her fingers, glistening in the morning sunlight, saw Rory trying to see how much blood there was, and wiped it quickly on her dress.

Blood was insidious now, a reminder of her very brief lifespan compared to Rory who would live the hundreds of years allotted to elves. In her old body, Hannah would have outlived him. Born vampires like her aged so slowly; they could live close to a thousand years if they were smart about it. Fledglings could potentially live forever - they never changed, bodies frozen in the place when they had been changed.

Now she was neither.

"Hannah?" Rory asked, and he stepped back, coming toward her, no doubt meaning to inspect the cut.

"I'm fine," she said in a low voice that bordered on sharpness, trying to remind herself that he meant well. His concern was for her well-being, because he loved her and wanted her to stay healthy, but sometimes, it didn't feel like that. It felt patronizing. Honestly, did he think her an idiot? Just because she had only spent a few weeks in this human body didn't mean she hadn't learned to respect its fragility.

She had spent her life feeding on humans; she knew how easily they could be broken. Even without her vampiric senses, she was still smart enough to take care of herself. Her body may be new, but she was not.

"Are you sure?" he asked, and she glared at him again.

"I said it's fine."

The elf returned her look. "Fine," he snapped. "Let's keep going." He started up the path at a brisk pace, and Hannah took advantage of her new body's longer legs to keep up with him. There were certainly some benefits to this new form. Though she didn't know if she would have chosen to live in a human body, it certainly was better than the alternative - the afterlife was not something Hannah was eager to explore just yet.

There were too many titillating mortal delights to discover.

And she would enjoy them, she decided, just as soon as they reached the top of this damn mountain, dropped off the package Rory had received in town, picked up anything the old widow wanted brought back down, and collected their pay for this little side jaunt.

They needed the money if they were going to continue south this way. It wasn't that they didn't have money - Rory had plenty of gold in his bag - but gold drew attention, the kind of attention they were trying to avoid. When the man at the inn mentioned this small favor he needed, it seemed simple enough. In exchange for a quick run up the mountain, an easy morning's travel to the top at the most, they would get three days of bed and board, plus a small fee in copper, coin that was much more common in these smaller villages in the middle of the country.

Hannah didn't think anyone from her father's castle was hunting them now, but it was better to be smart as they disappeared. They were conspicuous as it was, the elf and his human female, and people talked of them and about them wherever they went, though mostly about Rory. Apparently, they didn't get a lot of elves in the middle country. They were well off the beaten path, venturing into geography Hannah had only seen hinted at on old maps. Here in these small towns, even Hannah's blonde hair and pale skin garnered a few looks and whispers. The women here were dark haired and darker skinned, though not as dark as those who lived beyond the far southern desert. Hannah wondered what the people would look like when she and Rory finally stopped moving, when they would find a town and settle there.

Hannah pondered what that life would be like. Though he was her husband now, Rory had only ever been her road companion. They had never stayed in one place for longer than a few nights. She wondered what it would be like to live with Rory in one place, in a small home with a roof and a bed and just the two of them all the time. Hannah wondered what he would do in a town, what they would both do.

She had some skill as a blacksmith, recalled from her last body, though she would likely have to train this body's hands to go through the motions, and she would have to pay closer attention to her work. There had been times when, as a vampire, she had smashed her hand to a pulpy mess in a moment of inattention; then, the solution had been as simple as a fresh infusion of blood. Now, such an incident would cripple her for life. The idea still galled her sometimes.

She stared at Rory's back, watching the elf as he walked along the mountain path, shoulders straight and feet sure as they picked their way among the rocks. His arms swung loosely at his sides, arms that held her close to him at night, with hands that pressed against her in ways that made all of the minor inconveniences of this fragile mortal body worthwhile. There was the blood, of course, or lack thereof. She could kiss him and hold him, and just hear his heartbeat when she lay on his chest, and not feel the pull of his pulse calling to her from across the room, demanding that she taste him. It was oddly freeing to not want him like that anymore.

It made everything worthwhile.

She took a deep breath, something she thought she would never get tired of doing, relishing the feel of her chest filling with air, her breasts pressing against the front of her dress, and closed her eyes to truly appreciate the exhale. As a vampire, she could breathe if she wanted to, but she hadn't needed to. The relief from such a simple act in this human body was overwhelming; she was still savoring the feeling.

That was when her foot caught on something, and by the time she opened her eyes, she was already tumbling off the path, hitting a tree, and then sliding right off the edge of the mountain.

She heard Rory call her name, but then she was falling. She hit the ground hard on her upper back, remaining air pushed out of her lungs, and she gagged as her body continued to move. Her feet flopped over her head as she continued down, body picking up dirt and rocks as she rolled, occasionally bouncing off trees as she pinged from one obstacle to the next. She tried to reach out to grab something, anything, managed to snag a tree limb that slowed her for a second, and then the rest of her body slid sideways and out over empty air. She heard a disheartening crack from the branch she held, and then it let go, and she was falling, really falling. She managed to look around as a shelf of rock rushed passed her on one side, and then she hit water, body slamming into the frigid river like a solid wall.

She came to the surface in a sputter, all of her limbs flailing, nearly overcome with panic. *I can't swim, and now I'm going to drown - this body was the worst idea ever! Damn Klauden for putting me into it!*

Thoughts of her old friend calmed her, and she suddenly heard his voice in her head, the calm historian, soothing and patient. *Focus, chaivin. Take stock of the situation.*

She continued her frantic paddling, feet kicking uselessly into more water as she tried to look around. She was in the middle of a river, water spreading out on both sides to banks of rocky edges and mud crusted trees. The water was moving fast, the current dragging her along in its wake, her clothing heavy and trying to pull her under. She focused on her feet, using one foot to push the boot off of the other, and was relieved when she bobbed to the surface, one boot no longer weighing her down. She used her bare foot to shove her other boot free, and then she was floating more easily, her hair a tangle in her face as she tried to find a way out. She had to swim or try something better than this flailing in order to get to the edge, but which side?

She tried to find the horizon, the thin line of the setting sun a guide in the rush of water, and putting her back to it, she knew that Rory should be on her right side. She started kicking that way, moving with the current as best she could but trying to gain a few precious feet closer to the edge. The bank whooshed by, sometimes a rock shelf, sometimes a muddy swath, and she pressed her feet down, seeking the bottom. Her dress tangled around her legs, bunched up at her middle, then pulled down again, tugging her with it. She sputtered, gasping for breath before she went under and pumping with her arms to reach the surface again. Her heart was pounding, the sound echoing in her head under the water.

She became aware of another sound then, a roaring that went beyond her panic and the all too human blood rushing through her veins.

She kicked, face breaking the surface, and the roaring got louder.

Oh no.

Hannah knew that sound. When they approached the mountain, she and Rory had paused to admire the waterfalls. They had stood at the bottom and refilled their waterskins, taking their time as they soaked in the natural majesty of so much water falling from the top of the mountain.

It had been pretty.

Now, she was stuck in the flow of the river, fast approaching the cliff that formed the waterfall. Hannah cursed. She could see where the river ended up ahead. She could also make out what might be rocks that rose out of the middle of the water. Hannah started flailing back towards the middle, aiming for the rocks.

It was a small chance, but she'd take it.

Hannah spread her arms and legs wide, hoping to hit the rocks with at least some part of her body. The force of impact was enough to make her vision dance at the edges, and the water flung her sideways. Hannah held on to the edge, digging her fingers into the rock like claws as the rest of her body swung outward with the thrust of the water. Her weight pushed her down, and then she was dangling from the edge of a cliff, water roaring around her on both sides as she held on to rough edges above. She tried to pull herself up, but her arms were exhausted from fighting the water. She quickly gave that up to focus on other options. She peered down, trying to see what lay beneath her. There was water, yes, and fog from the spray, but she was pretty sure that there was an outcropping of rock far below her.

Her fingers were screaming in protest, her fingernails pulling as she gripped the rock. She had to let go.

I will fall, she thought clearly, and on the heels of that, *and that's alright.*

She conjured the words to the spell with a desperation she didn't know she had in her, spewed them forth just as her fingers let go, and then she was falling, but softly, gently, her feet touching down on a small outcropping of rock far below. She let the magic help her to her knees, then fell forward, aching hands held tight to her chest, and curled up. She lay on her side for a moment, just breathing. When she opened her eyes, she saw that the slab of rock she occupied was actually the entrance to a cave. She scooted further into the darkness, away from the biting cold of the water spray, and curled up once more.

She just needed to sleep for a moment. After that, she could take stock.

A small voice deep inside her head cried out at this thought, but Hannah only understood the very last word. "Light."

Yes, she thought dazedly, as the darkness enveloped her, *light would be nice.*

She knew the words, mumbled them through numb lips, but by the time the spell blazed forth, she was already unconscious.

***

Rory heard the sound of Hannah stumbling, her boot dragging against something on the ground. He turned around as she made a surprised sound, and he saw her tilt dangerously to the edge of the path. He reached for her, her sleeve grazing his fingers as she tumbled, and then she was beyond his reach. He watched in horror as she first slammed into a tree, skidded to the side, and then twisted over the edge and dropped out of sight. He was moving at once, hands grasping for tree limbs to steady himself as he followed her path, holding tight to a final tree as he leaned forward over the edge.

He heard a thump and more noise, and the hand that had been squeezing his chest released a fraction. At least she hadn't fallen very far. Listening to the sound of Hannah's jolting trip down the mountain though, he wondered if it would matter. He could make out the motion of her tumbling form below him, sliding from tree to tree, hitting, he was pretty certain, every single one on the way, and then he saw her fast approaching yet another edge.

Damn the luck!

He couldn't see where that one led from his perch up, so he gave a quick prayer to the gods and let go of the tree, trusting his instincts to help him keep his feet. He landed solidly, but the soft dirt quickly gave way beneath his boots. He was ready for that though, leaping deftly down the incline from rocks to the base of trees, this time stepping lightly on a stump, there bouncing quickly off of a mound of twisted roots. He saw Hannah's bag, abandoned against a flattened bush, and snagged it as he ran passed. He was making good time, halfway to the drop-off when he watched Hannah go over the side.

He listened for the sound of her landing, his own heart pounding in his ears along with the same litany of *No! No! No!* in his mind, and then there was a splash. Rory's heart sank further than he thought possible. He ran the last paces to the edge, catching himself on a tree limb as he slid to a stop before going over. He looked out into the empty space, then down, far down, to the rushing water below.

Hannah had fallen into the damn river. He really should have taken the time to teach her to swim. It hadn't seemed like an important thing; they could swim when they reached the place they decided to settle in. Besides, the water was still far too cold for any fun. A few more weeks and farther travel to the south would make the lessons far more enjoyable. Clearly, he had been a fool to wait. He should have known Hannah would need to learn as soon as possible. She was always getting herself into ridiculous situations.

He scanned the cliff, hands quickly pulling at vines and roots, judging his path down to the river's edge. He could see the cliff dipped in underneath him, but he was fairly certain he could climb down if luck was with him. He knelt at the edge, let Hannah's bag hang below him for a second, then dropped it, not waiting to see if it landed on the edge and missed the water. He grabbed hold of the nearest root and started over the edge, confident hands finding grips along the way. There was a moment when he thought this was probably a bad idea, especially when the root in his hand sprang free with a twang and left him dangling from one hand. But then his feet swayed to the rock wall, finding purchase among the nooks and crannies there, and soon he was skidding and sliding his way to the ground below.

He saw Hannah's bag in the mud near of the edge of the water, scooped it up, and began hurrying down along the river, scanning the surface for Hannah. Had she been able to stay afloat? Or had the fall knocked her unconscious and was she, even now, drowning?

Rory forced himself to calm down, feet sure on the ground as he moved, eyes scanning from side to side. He caught motion far ahead and saw a small shape flailing. He doubled his speed, ears registering what he had been trying not to think about - the roar of the waterfalls ahead.

She couldn't swim; he knew that for sure - but maybe she could paddle to the edge and get out of the water in time. Judging by the swift current rushing by as he ran alongside, Rory doubted it. He was a strong swimmer, and he didn't know if he would be able to fight the water in this river.

If she had her old strength, sure, she would have been able to get out just fine. Of course, if she were in her old impervious body, neither water nor cliffs nor any amount of bodily harm - save fire - would have been able to stop her. Now, though, she was human. Fragile.

He knew it was better this way, since now they could actually be together without her turning him into a fledgling, but right then, he would have given anything for Hannah's old body.

He kept his eyes on the bobbling form, feet finding purchase on rocks and fallen trees and mud as he followed. He was almost near her when she bounced into a rock at the edge, and he saw her slide slowly over the edge. He yelled in frustration, then slid along the rocks, trying to get a better view of the falls from the side. He couldn't see the water at the bottom through the mist, but he didn't actually see Hannah fall down there. Maybe she held on somehow?

He picked his way carefully along the rocks that marked the cliff's edge to a tree that hung out over the opening. He dropped Hannah's bag, using both hands to shimmy out on a limb to see more of the falls. Through the misty water haze, he saw a small form dangling from the cliff in the middle of the falls. As he watched, the hands let go, but instead of plummeting into the water, Hannah dropped slowly, the glow of magic surrounding her entire body. She landed on a small outcropping of rock, then collapsed on the ground. Rory was certain for a terrifying moment that she was dead, the spell some kind of contingency magic designed to take care of her body in the event of her death. But then the body moved, slumped to one side, and slid forward on the shelf, away from the water and the edge. Another glow surrounded her, and Rory recognized her light spell. She didn't move again, but the light illuminated the opening of a cave beyond where she lay.

If he could get to her, he could help her. He might not have Klauden's gift of healing magic, but he knew how to bind wounds, knew how to keep people alive, and he could do that. Hannah was alive. It was enough.

He just had to get to her.

He judged the distance to the rock that she had fallen from. He couldn't jump from where he was, and the water was too swift for him to swim across from the edge. He could try, but he didn't think it was possible. He could try swimming from farther upstream, but even then, in such a strong current, he wasn't sure he could hit the mark perfectly. More likely, he'd go sailing off the edge with the water - and he didn't have a soft fall spell to ease his landing.

He had rope. He could tie it to the edge of this tree, climb down, and swing himself over. He had read stories as a child of the great jungle elves who swung on vines from tree to tree. It was crazy, but he had to try. His hands were strong. He could hold on. And the tree was sturdy enough.

It was the only plan he had.

It took him a few moments to shimmy back to the edge, secure his belongings and Hannah's bag tightly to his body, then climb back out on the tree, rope in hand. He tied a knot to the edge, then a loop at the bottom of the rope and knots every few feet. His grip was good, but the rope would be wet. He would slide all over the place. Saying a quick prayer to whatever gods would listen, Rory slipped off the limb on to the rope, feet gaining good purchase on the knots as he moved down. When he was about level with the ledge, he started to sway, kicking his body back and forth to gain enough momentum to cross the gap between him and the ledge. The water hurt when he swung into it, but he got enough range of motion to actually kick off the cliff under the tree, propelling himself through the spray and onto the ledge. He wanted to hold on to the rope - it was their only certain escape route - but it wasn't long enough, and he could feel it trying to pull him back out over empty space. He let go, falling in a heap on the ledge behind Hannah, one foot sliding back over empty air before he fell forward on top of her. His weight on her caused her to gasp, a loud "oof!" that reassured him. If she could make a sound like that, she was still alive.

If she was still alive, everything would be alright.

***

Hannah woke to someone touching her face. The feeling was warm, a soothing contrast to the cold numbness she felt everywhere else. She thought her body might start to hurt soon, the emptiness a promise of pain to come, but she lay still, relishing the warmth bathing her face.

She opened her eyes, and Rory was looking down at her, a cloth in his hand as he wiped her cheek. A relieved smile spread across his face as he saw she was awake, breaking through the mask of worry. Hannah had a moment of complete dislocation - she had been here before, lying on her back as Rory wiped her face, and she had been wounded then, aching with bloodfever - but that had been months ago, in another body, next to a different river. Rory hadn't known yet what she was.

Movement at her side brought her back to the present. Glancing down, she saw that Rory was holding one of her hands gently in his, her fingers resting on his palm. Her fingers were numb, but she could see that they were a reddish purple, and her nails were ragged, some lifted from her fingers, and one completely torn off her ring finger. *That is really going to hurt when I can feel again*, she thought.

She noticed that she could actually see and looked around for the light source. She was lying on her back in a small cave, a little fire burning brightly against the wall near her feet, and the roar she had thought was inside her head was actually the sound of the waterfall outside. She looked at the opening of the cave and the ledge beyond. A small amount of late afternoon light peeked in around the water.

"What ...happened?" she managed to say through cracked lips.

"What do you remember?" he asked softly, laying her hand down on her chest and pushing her hair out of her face and behind her ears, fingers resting against the line of her jaw.

"I tripped," she said, and laughed, the sound choked as it came out. Rory cupped her cheek, holding her as she coughed. "I'm pretty sure I hit every single tree on the way down."

Rory laughed then too, tension going out of him as he released her. "I thought the same thing!"

"Well," she decided, "if I'm going to fall off a mountain, I suppose I should do it right."

"Oh Hannah," he breathed, and he was near her again, body cradling hers as she giggled helplessly. Feeling was creeping back into her hands, her fingers singing with fire, and she moaned a little.

"Here," Rory said, producing a small glass bottle from his bag. "I didn't want to give it to you until you woke up, but it will take away some of the pain."

Hannah sat up in his arms and allowed him to tip the bottle into her mouth. She took a few small sips of the bitter liquid, coughed, and then lay back down. Rory stared at her. She could feel him taking stock of her injuries, waited for the inevitable anger at her clumsiness. Though she could see the worried frustration in him, he didn't say anything, instead watching her silently.

"How bad am I?" Hannah whispered, feeling the liquid steal through her limbs, pain vanishing in a haze of warm drowsiness. The whiskey always worked quickly in this body. Rory had given her other sips as they traveled - when she nearly broke her shin falling onto a boulder's edge, when she pulled her wrist out of joint trying to lift weight that her old body could have handled easily, when she knocked her shoulder out of alignment that time they fought those goblins. Hannah had to admit that maybe Rory had reason to worry so much about her, but she resisted the urge to add, "this time."

Her husband shook his head, eyes closing as he took a deep breath. "Not bad, considering," Rory replied, looking at her again, his face unreadable. "Your hands are the worst of it. You have some bruises and scrapes, but you should recover. You are very lucky to be alive." He paused, hands rubbing her shoulders through the damp material of her dress. Hannah felt the pull of sleep, soft and demanding. She closed her eyes. "You're so cold, Hannah. Let's get you out of those wet clothes."

Hannah mumbled something in response, but then she was dreaming of warmth and quiet.

The next time she opened her eyes, the fire had burned down to a low glow. Rory's metal lantern sat near her head, a small pinprick of light in the dimness of the cave. She was curled up against him, their bare skin pressed against each other, his cloak serving as a blanket for them both. Hannah wondered how long she had been naked, and she spied her dress spread out next to the remains of the fire, presumably drying. Rory's clothes were also laid out, and she ran a hand along the smooth planes of his chest and hips. Her fingers hurt, but it was distant still. In the light of the lantern, she could see that the redness of cold had vanished, replaced by dark purple that would likely bruise. Her fingernails were a disaster, though she could see that Rory must have trimmed the worst edges while she was out. She could see the raw exposed flesh from under her nails, but nothing was bleeding, so that was a good sign. She tried to flex her fingers, felt the skin tight at her knuckles and the pain sharp, but not unbearable.

Looking down at herself, she saw she had a few darkening bruises on her ribs and arms, and her face ached like she may have a black eye, but Rory had been right. Her hands had taken the worst of it.

She had been so incredibly lucky.

She was still marveling at divine blessings when Rory stirred under her, eyes opening lazily to look at her.

"Hey," he said, arm coming around her back to pull her close, but gently, mindful of her bruises.

"Hey," she replied.

"How..." he paused, not wanting to finish the question. She could feel the tension in him as he pushed some strong emotion aside. Instead he looked around the small cave. "It's not bad, you know."

Hannah cocked an eyebrow. "What isn't bad?"

"Well, all things considered, this is quite cozy. Fire, waterfall, small cave, all alone in the wilderness with the woman I love..."

Hannah tapped him playfully on the arm with the palm of her hand, careful not to touch anything with her fingers. "Trapped in a tiny cave behind a waterfall after nearly falling to my death...yeah, definitely cozy."

His hand started rubbing her shoulder, and then her neck, long fingers pressing delightfully into all of her favorite places. She gave him a look. "Seriously?"

He grinned. "It's not like we have anywhere else to be right now. We're not leaving in the dark. And you seem to be feeling fine."

"My hands aren't so fine," she commented, pressing close to him, but carefully.

"No, they will take a bit to heal." He pressed his hand against hers softly, her hand small in his, but not as small as her old body had been. "But you will recover," he paused, then added, "and I am thankful for it." His hand began a slow but determined journey up her arm and around to her back.

She quirked an eyebrow at him, pulling away a little bit to see him. "What do you mean, thankful? I'm hurt. I'm lucky I didn't die today."

"I know," he agreed, and kissed her, mouth demanding as his hands tried to hold all of her at once. When he finally pulled away for breath, he stayed close to her, whispering, "Wounds remind you that you are still alive, and that is always a good thing."

"Always?" she murmured, the warmth of him so close and tempting, his body pressed tight against hers.

"Always," he replied, and then there was no more talking for a time.

In the morning, they scoured the cave for an exit strategy. Hannah had taken another small sip of Rory's painkiller, the fire in her fingertips retreating for the moment, but she was still very careful not to touch things. She had sat quietly that morning while Rory slept, her hands carefully flipping pages in her spellbook, mindful not to let any water splash the magic book. She knew it would survive just about anything, but she was careful, and she slid it gently back into her bag with reverence. Rory had been restless when he woke, getting dressed quickly to scan their surroundings in the morning light. She joined Rory where he stood at the edge, peering down into the mist below.

She glanced from where they stood to the tree that grew out over the cliffs. "You really swung across that chasm on a rope?" she asked again, marveling at the elf she had married. "I really wish I could have seen that!"

"It was a damn foolish thing to do," he admitted, shrugging, "but I couldn't think of another way to get to you." The tension in him was back, the lines of his shoulders tight as he stepped away from the ledge and went back to his search.

Hannah stepped close to the edge, leaning over to peer into the depths. Rory's hand grabbed her shoulder from behind and pulled her back, and she repressed the urge to snap at him. Did he really think she would fall again? "We could jump," she said, if only to see his horrified reaction. He saw she was joking and shook his head with a sigh of frustration.

"We could try to climb up or swing over to the side," Rory offered, then looked at her hands, face darkening at the sight of her raw flesh. "But you're not climbing like that. You can't hold on to anything."

Hannah pursed her lips, considering. She could tell him how they could get out of this place now, but she decided to wait. Watching him stew as he tried to figure something out was worth it. He deserved it for not trusting her.

She heard him sigh heavily inside the cave, the frustration building, and she relented. "Rory," she said, but then he was beside her, jerking her close to him and kissing her soundly as he tugged her away from the edge. As often was the case, her husband had decided to distract himself with other things.

"Maybe we could just stay here for a few more days until you heal up," he suggested.

She pushed him away. "Cute," she said, but she saw how he looked at her face in the morning light, guessing that she must be bruised badly around her eyes. He was buzzing a bit at the edges, clearly angry but trying not to say anything, distracting himself by kissing her instead. He wasn't getting out of this so easily. She pressed her hands to his chest, pushing him back against the cliff wall to the side of the cave opening. "Out with it," she demanded. "What is wrong?"

Her looked away from her, face blank. "I don't know what you mean."

"Like hell," she snarled. "You're pissed at something. Tell me why."

His face broke, and the annoyance showed through. He gestured at their surroundings, and then glared at her. "Look, Hannah. I'm glad you're alive. I am. Truly." He looked around again, shaking his head, then back at her. "But I just wish maybe you'd be more careful so we wouldn't find ourselves in these kinds of situations."

There. He had said it. Hannah felt the heat rise in her face, the throb of her eye pumping in time to her heartbeat. She thought if she were still a vampire, she would have sensed the blood rising inside. She could see a matching red glow creeping up Rory's neck.

"Do you honestly think I fell off a mountain on purpose?" she asked, voice quietly menacing.

"No. But I do think that you need to pay more attention to things. You should be dead. The only reason you're not is because you were damned lucky. And your magic - " he stopped abruptly, staring at her, some realization hitting him hard.

She nodded at him, feeling the surge of satisfaction as she watched him finally get it. "Yes," she said. "My magic."

He looked around again, then back at her. "Can you get us out of here?"

She nodded. "Of course. What do you think I was doing all morning while you slept?"

He ignored the barb. "Then let's go," he said, pushing passed her to collect his bag. Hannah stood where she was.

"No."

"No?" He turned to face her, face questioning.

She shook her head. "We're not finished here."

Rory looked up to the water above them. "We should have reached that widow yesterday. She'll be waiting on us now."

"And she can wait," Hannah said.

"For what?"

"For you to apologize for being a pompous ass."

Rory stared at her, red creeping across both cheeks, chest moving a little as he took deep breaths. "How have I been an ass?"

"Look at you, so angry at me because I tripped and fell."

"You are constantly tripping and falling," he reminded her. "You run around in that body like it's your old one, and you're going to get yourself killed. I'm an ass for worrying about you?"

"No, you're an ass because you don't trust me." She closed the gap between them, hands pressing against his face and cupping his cheeks. "I know this body is fragile. I'm learning to take care of it. I could do that a lot better if you stopped babying me."

"Babying you? Hannah, you fell off the mountain because you weren't paying attention!"

"Yes, and I survived!"

"You survived because you were incredibly lucky!"

"I survived because I was lucky, but also because of my magic. I am not helpless, Rory. I am not just this jejune slave girl," she gestured at her body. "I'm still *me* in here. You don't seem to remember that."

"I see you," he said.

"Do you? Because it only *just* occurred to you that I could use my magic to get us out of here. In my old body, you wouldn't have doubted it for a minute. You would rely on me. But now, you just see her, this clumsy, tall human who trips and falls and hurts herself."

"I don't want to lose you." His voice was quiet, his face ashamed.

"And I appreciate that, but right now, you're barely seeing me at all." Hannah moved away from him to the other side of the ledge. She could feel the spray of the water on her face, and she turned away from it, glancing back at where Rory stood, still pressed against the wall.

Rory seemed about to say something, then stopped himself, staring hard at her instead. When he did speak, his voice was calm, considering. "When I saw you go over the edge yesterday, I thought you were dead," he paused, chest hitching a little, "and I never want to feel that way again." Hannah tried to imagine what it might feel like, watching Rory disappear over the edge of a cliff and remembered watching him fight in the tournament back in her father's castle. She had thought he would die then.

Rory's face was red, eyes dark with remembered emotion. "But then I saw you hanging on to the edge, and when you fell that time, I was sure, sure you were gone." He shook his head then, a small grin replacing the fear. "Then I saw the magic, and for a moment, I thought it was a contingency, like Malbrek used, a spell designed to go off in the event of your death. But it wasn't anything like that." He stepped over to her.

"You used your magic. Disoriented, wounded, and dangling from a waterfall, you used your magic to save yourself."

Hannah nodded, wanting to make a dismissive sound. Why wouldn't she use her magic to save herself? But she waited for him to continue. "I know you, Hannah. Not this body, but you. Truly."

Hannah smirked at him. "You say that now, sure, but what about the next time something happens? Will you depend on me or will you rush to defend me from myself?"

He didn't answer right away. "I will...try," he said eventually.

"Ok," she said, accepting the compromise. "That's all I ask."

"But if you insist on throwing yourself off cliffs, I am going to pester you about taking better care of yourself."

"Deal," she said, reaching out a hand. He took hers gently, letting her fingers rest on his palm. "Now hold on to me. I'm going to get us out of here."

Rory reached out to grab both of her shoulders, and she recited the spell carefully, allowing the magic to pour out of her. The transportation spell wasn't something she did often - it required a great deal of concentration - but one moment they were standing on the rock ledge, and the next they were standing on the mountain path. Rory held on to her as they opened their eyes, and Hannah could see the spot a few feet ahead where she had stumbled. There was a root lying in the path, a small thing really, but enough to trip an unsuspecting foot. She waited for her head to clear from the magic, felt the low thrum in her temples that signaled an impending headache, and gently took Rory's hand, leading him up the path, careful to step over the root this time.

Rory moved up next to her, keeping pace easily, but he wasn't watching her every move, and Hannah felt a small surge of hope. Maybe he really would stop worrying about her all the time.

The combination of magic and wounds caught up to her before they reached the widow's house, and Hannah stopped, squatting on her haunches to take a break. She took a drink of water from her waterskin, a hand to her forehead. She was still wounded, and the spell had been a big one. She really wanted to sleep in a bed as soon as possible.

Rory looked at her, but didn't say anything.

"I could use a drink," she admitted. "Even some of that whiskey you have. It's awful stuff, but it would be nice right about now." She felt the shrieking pain of her body, this terribly weak body. "Or maybe just a good knife to put me out of my misery."

Rory grinned at her, hands at his belt. "I'm pretty sure I have a blade handy," he replied. "Would you prefer a stiletto or the longsword?"

"I don't know," she answered. "Would you trust me with either while walking on this path?"

Rory smiled at her. "I trust you, Hannah. I will always trust you."

About JM Paquette

JM Paquette hails from upstate New York, so she misses the snow, but not the shoveling, and now lives in Florida, where she hates the heat, but not the beach. She has an embarrassingly large comic book collection that is only shamed by her ever growing horde of cheesy romance novels, and she openly admits to being both a fantasy enthusiast and a roleplaying aficionado—both of which have earned her solid stamps on her Geek Card. She lives in Clearwater with her husband, her daughter, her big-boned dog, and a cat who occasionally appears at mealtimes.

Connect with JM:
Facebook.com/AuthorJMPaquette
Email: authorjmpaquette@gmail.com

Other books by JM Paquette
Klauden's Ring (Book One of the Klauden's Ring Saga)
On the Verge (Anthology)
Behind the Veil (Anthology)
The Death of Jimmy (Anthology)
Into the Abyss (Anthology)

The Peanut Memo

By Dalia Lance

The sun was still warming the breeze as it began the decent into the horizon. The waves crashed along the shore of my favorite secluded part of North Beach. I looked out at the ocean and imagined the endless possibilities my life would hold. After all, when you're married to a millionaire the world is your playground.

A smile crept across my face when I felt his hands run down my arms and wrap around my waist. He held me against him and I shuddered. Marcus was everything I had ever dreamed of. He was tall, over six feet, with dark hair and piercing cobalt blue eyes. Fit from his countless outdoor activities, he had a smile to make any woman swoon.

I felt him kiss my neck and then whisper into my ear, "Mr. Sands would like to see you."

"Wait, what?" I said, startled.

"Mr. Sands would like to discuss the email he said he sent you this morning. Are you drunk or something?" It was Stephanie.

I took a deep breath, disappointed to find I was not on the beach with the amazing Marcus Rex about to tell me he loved me. Instead, I was in my office, staring at a calendar that depicted the sunset I was wishing I was standing in front of. I looked up into the face of possibly the worst assistant anyone could ask for.

Stephanie had been a transfer when Marken Imaging and Rex Graphics merged. She had been the assistant for the Human Resource officer who left when news of the merge was leaked, taking a generous severance package with her and leaving me to inherit Stephanie. She had absolutely gotten the better end of the deal.

Stephanie could manage to screw up the simplest of tasks, and the alphabet seemed to elude her when it came to filing. She also seemed impervious to any correction or discipline, like a human version of The Cat in the Hat.

Normally I would hear the clicking of her stilettos coming down the hall towards my office, giving me plenty of warning of her arrival. Stephanie, it seemed, felt the more you hated your job, the less you had to wear to it. She wore the clicking heels each day with a skirt that appeared to have been purchased in the children's section based on its length. I wondered if I was becoming immune to her. The thought was terrifying.

Appraising Stephanie's outfit, I saw that she was wearing thigh-high black leather boots with rubber soles. That explained the no clacking. Her shirt, which was loose and belted at the hips, barely covered the parts of her pants normally would, and the tights she presently had on didn't. I debated asking if she had decided to wear undergarments, but thought the better of it.

I shook my head with a sigh. I could point out the dress code violations, but it would only end in frustration on my part and the likelihood of Stephanie wearing a scarf as a shirt tomorrow.

"Tell Mr. Sands I will be with him shortly," I said.

Stephanie said, "K" and left the office looking as if I had annoyed her by simply existing, which I'm sure I did.

It was looking to be the beginning of another normal Monday for me in the Human Resource Department of Marken-Rex Imaging. Sometimes I thought I hated the place more than Stephanie did.

Besides the imaginary trip to the beach, the day had started with only three minor incidents, missing time and/or vacation pay from the previous weeks' paychecks; you know the easy stuff. After five years, I could recognize the easy stuff.

Still, when I had gotten away with only these hiccups to begin the day, and I was able to drink my first cup of coffee without interruptions, I should have known the other shoe had failed to drop.

I clicked open my email to check through the various inane requests I received every day from those employees who apparently thought I had been hired to resolve only those issues that affected them. I skimmed through the spam of sexual enhancements and cheap airfares, the ones the IT department swore there is no cure for, and I found it. When I saw the name in bold in my inbox, my hand twitched on the keyboard, desperately wanting to click the delete button.

Brian Sands. I hated the man.

The subject of his email was "Allergies."

I began to get a headache. I knew that whatever his email contained was going to ruin my whole day, and potentially the week.

After Brian's last email, I had been forced to rewrite the policy on bereavement leave to better define who qualified as a relative. Brian had taken bereavement time when Dale Earnhart died because he felt Dale was "like a brother" to him. Brian had never met Mr. Earnhart, which it seemed did not matter because Brian said that he "felt as close to him as he would a real brother if he had one."

He took all five days paid to "grieve". Meanwhile, it was four days of handbook rewrites and redistribution. Four days that I would never get back. That was just the last one. There were three other rewrites before then. One very memorable change was to no longer allow employees to cook popcorn in the microwaves because the smell can "linger" causing "nausea" to those who are not fans of the tasty treat. These annoying limitations in our workplace were all thanks to one Mr. Brian Sands.

I hated this man.

I knew that whatever "this" was, it was not going away. First, I would have to determine if he had copied anyone else in his email. That always led to having the same conversation over again. If there were three managers copied, there would be at least three separate conversations with me explaining the exact same thing with three separate people giving me their "expert" advice on how best to do my job. I opened the email.

To Whom It May Concern:

I have come to a realization about a life and death danger that I am experiencing in the work place. I have severe peanut/tree nut allergies that are life threatening. I have noticed that several employees snack at their desk, and those employees eating peanut/tree nut products are then handling files and documents that I could come into contact with. I respectfully request that this threat to my life be eliminated and a safe environment be created for my situation. I look forward to your timely reply.

B. Sands

I hated this man.

I re-read the email at least three more times. In less than four minutes my entire day had been destroyed. A new record.

I stared at the screen for a little bit; at least he had not copied anyone else. I had some breathing room. I buzzed Stephanie and asked her to send Mr. Sands in.

A couple of minutes later the door opened and Mr. Sands stood in the threshold to my office. He looked like a rodent. He was a smaller man, balding, and wore a polo in a dingy grey color and khakis; they clashed. It was his beady small dark brown eyes and pointed nose that gave the full rat like effect.

"Mr. Sands, please sit. What can I do for you today?" I asked.

"Ms. Tanner, did you receive my email?" he asked in his squeaky voice.

I maintained my composure. When you work in any capacity in HR you have to be able to smile and keep your composure, even if you truly want to murder the person sitting across from you. I have come to understand that is not only frowned upon but illegal.

I had taken several training courses in the last few years to keep on the cutting edge of all things HR, and to have an excuse to be out of the office for up to three days at a time. One of the instructors had said to keep a journal of any negative thoughts you had during the day as a way to release your frustrations without taking them out on those you are supposed to be helping. I began to write in one that night until I realized that if the journal was ever found it would be the best piece of evidence in a trial that an angry ex-employee could find.

I cleared my throat. "Yes, Mr. Sands. I did have the opportunity to review the email you sent and I realize this matter is of the utmost importance. I will be working on it today to have a speedy resolution." I crossed my fingers out of view that this would be all it would take, and this vile creature would leave my office. I wasn't so lucky.

As Mr. Sands rose to leave he turned around and said, "I hope it is soon. I would hate to inconvenience anyone by dying at work."

With tight lips I simply nodded as he left.

I hate that man.

I decided to do some research. If this was an actual disability, maybe there were sometimes loopholes; not in this case, however. After two hours of reading confusing government regulations and case studies on the internet, I discovered that I needed to do something to prevent the death of this afflicted employee. I really wanted to go eat a peanut butter sandwich and shake his hand.

I printed off all the information on the subject and began work on the office memorandum. I titled it *Severe Allergies in the Workplace.*

I spent about an hour writing, proofreading, and editing out phrases such as "whiney pansy boy" and changing them to "fellow employee."

When I finally had a memo that covered all the points of the case law, I needed to go to the President's office. He was final approval on all matters regarding legal situations in HR. He had no formal training, but because he had the title President on his door he was an "expert."

It was 12:52 pm. I realized I hadn't eaten yet and four cups of coffee only get you so far. It might have been six. Food was still needed so I made a detour and headed to the Café, which was really a cafeteria but the higher ups felt that sounded too much like high school or a hospital, so they renamed it.

With the newly typed memo in hand I pushed open the door to the Café with a little too much zeal and knocked a drink right out of Marcus Rex's hand and onto his shirt. I cringed.

I stood stunned at the scene that unfolded in front of me. I envisioned Marcus with his shirt wet from the rain we were both running though, and then I pulled it off his muscular chest as we warmed ourselves in front of fire in a log cabin...

What the hell is wrong with me, I thought. I am fantasizing about fireplaces and cabins and I just spilled...something all over our VP of Product Development. He's an owner to boot!

"Oh my god Mr. Rex, I am so sorry..." I started blathering. I am sure I looked like I was hyperventilating.

"It is ok, it is only tea," Marcus said reaching out and putting his hand on my shoulder.

His voice was deep and sensual and when his hand touched me I almost screamed out.

My crush on Marcus Rex began at the first company meeting after the merger of the two firms. Rex Imaging was one of the many ventures of the Rex family, and Marcus, one of three brothers, had been the head of product development at Rex Imaging for the last 4 years. Many had wondered why, since he was beyond wealthy, he would take a position at one of the companies and not be President or CEO. It turned out that he loved creating things and making a difference. All of this made him even more attractive.

"I'm fine, thank you...I...tea did you say? I can get your shirt cleaned or a new one, I think, unless it's more than $700 then just take this week's paycheck..." Words were tumbling out of my mouth and I couldn't stop them.

"Sarah, stop." He was smiling and it was amazing. "It is fine really. It's just a shirt." Marcus Rex knew my name? I felt the flush in my cheeks turn a deeper red.

"Where were you headed in such a hurry?" he asked.

"I was taking the Peanut Memo to the President and getting a snack." I sounded like an idiot.

"Your what memo?" he asked smiling again.

"Peanut. It's a memo about peanuts... the life threatening kind..." I was trying to pull it together and I was failing horribly. When I imagined this moment, which I had many times, I hadn't sounded like such a moron. Isn't it amazing how when you fantasize something you have the perfect level of confidence and ability to say exactly what you mean to? Now, in front of the biggest crush I had ever had in my life, instead of having a titillating indiscretion at the office, I felt like a middle schooler all over again.

Marcus was chuckling. Seeing my reaction, he composed himself and asked, "Well then, with such an important memo that can mean the life or death in the hands of peanuts, can I possibly escort you to the Café? Purely in the interest of keeping you safe, of course, from the peanuts."

I stood there stunned for a moment. Did he just ask to escort me to the Café? Was he doing it because he felt bad for the confused stammering HR girl? He knew me by name. That was good. Then again, I had said nothing intelligent since literally bumping into him. So I said the only thing I could think of, "But your shirt?"

He looked down, and a small frown played across his features. Before he could say anything else and before I stuck my foot even father into my mouth, I looked down at my non-existent watch. "I better run. Mr. Marken, is waiting." I turned and hurried away letting the door close behind me.

WOW, I thought to myself as I boarded the elevator for the top floor. That could not have ended any worse if I had tried. I was still shaking my head as I exited the elevator and headed to the President's off.

I only waited forty or so minutes before the President's secretary waved me in. My stomach was growling loudly. I hoped he would look at it for about three minutes without actually reading it. He did that often, and it guaranteed my only having to be there long enough for him to put up the show of being in control of what I published to the staff.

Mr. Marken was a part owner and had been the President of Marken Imaging. He had retained his position when the companies merged. He stood at 5 foot 9 inches tall, his hair was a sandy blonde, now graying, that he kept a little longer than most men in his position. He wore pastel colored shirts with bright ties and his skin was the kind of wrinkled you get from too much sun.

When I glanced at the clock on his wall, five minutes had passed. He was leaning back in his oversized executive chair. He had on his reading glasses.

Seven minutes; this was not a good sign. He let out a long sigh, sweat glistening off his brow, pulled off his reading glasses, and set the memo on his desk. He asked, "Can we fire this guy?"

This was going to end badly.

I began to explain the legal ramifications of the situation when he waved his hand in the air to shush me. "I asked if we can fire him. Can we?" he asked me again, raising his voice.

"No," was all I could say. I despised being shushed.

"Why not?" he retorted.

I took a long deep breath. "I cannot fire someone for being allergic to peanuts."

I wondered about the merits of having someone be the final say on all things HR who could not even think that to its logical conclusion.

He looked around and then looked back at the memo for what seemed like another ten minutes. I was only guessing. My stomach sounded as if there were an alien trying to claw its way out, and I was beginning to feel the same way, so I was in no hurry to look up and find out how long I had really been sitting there.

"Did you know I was a diabetic?" he finally said. I did know, but had discovered long before that he liked to retell these types of things and got annoyed when I knew a fact on which he placed so much importance, regardless of the countless times I had told him about HR rules regarding privacy.

"No, I was not aware of that," I replied, lying.

"Being a diabetic means I have to regulate my blood sugar. You know this of course?" he asked and did not wait for my answer before he continued, "In order to maintain the proper amount of blood sugar, I have been instructed by my physician to consume nuts as a snack daily. Do I have to stop eating nuts and possibly threaten my life for this yahoo?" His face was flushed now. I sat there trying to decide what the correct thing to do or say was. "Call the lawyer. Find a way to fire this guy." His final words and he waved me out.

This was turning out to possibly be the worst day of my life.

I returned to my office. I hoped I would pass Stephanie and she could go grab me something to snack on. This notion was farfetched because she was of course not at her desk. I wasn't even sure if she was still at work. I was sure she was still clocked in.

2:04pm.

I called the lawyer, Adler Fintly. He was the one, if not the only, person I interacted with that understood what it was like to be me. I explained the situation to him and after him saying several times, "You can't do that," we came up with a solution. I loved this man.

I rewrote the memo and took it back upstairs, this time with a requisition form attached.

3:17pm.

This time when I arrived at the President's office his secretary gestured for me to go right in. She looked a little worried, but I wasn't sure if that was for her or me. When I saw Mr. Marken's face I knew it was for me.

He appeared to still be worked up. I handed him the revisions and the form and took a seat.

He put his glasses on and looked at me over the top of the frame. "So did you find a way to let him go?" he asked, barely restraining himself.

"No, Mr. Fintly agreed with me. We cannot fire him." I paused. "I believe that I found a solution for the situation, and Mr. Fintly agrees that it is the most legally sound." He could not argue with that when I had spent $800 to be able to utter those words.

He spent some time reading the memo, about five times as far as I could tell. He finally made a snorting noise, initialed his part of the form, handed both papers back to me and waved me out again.

I took the requisition form to the supply area and told the supervisor, Mark, that it was a rush and I needed the items first thing the next day. He nodded and said he would see what he could do.

I headed back to my office after stopping by the break room to grab a cup of coffee and a snack. First, I sent the newly revised "Severe Allergies" policy to Stephanie to distribute and revise the Employee Handbook. Then I opened the email from Brian and typed my reply.

Dear Mr. Sands,

Thank you for bringing the situation regarding your allergy to my attention. After speaking with legal council and conducting a review of our present facilities, it has been determined that the total removal of peanuts/tree nuts from the work environment is not feasible. It has come to light that there are several employees with medical conditions that require the consumption of nuts.

In an effort to accommodate your situation however, I have notified all employees that they need to wash their hands after the consumption of nuts or nut products. There is a Handbook amendment that you should receive a copy of shortly.

I am also glad to inform you that we have purchased a supply of surgical masks and gloves for you to wear while at work to prevent any accidental exposure to the harmful substances. We hope these will assist you in being able to take full precautions. You can pick up an ample supply from HR tomorrow morning.

Please let me know if I can be of further assistance.

Sarah Tanner
Human Resources

I clicked send and printed a copy for his file.
4:52 pm.

My stomach growled again, and I picked up my snack, took a few bites and finally began to calm my stomach, and my stress level. I imagined Brian in his cubical with a mask and gloves and I couldn't help but grin a little. Although the day had been horrible I was able to end it with a small win for me.

I began clicking through the emails that had stacked up in my inbox when Stephanie opened my office door startling me again, and said "This came for you." She set a basket on my desk that had a big ribbon around it, full of tasty treats and a bottle of whiskey.

I opened the card and it read, "Figured you needed this. How about dinner? I will bring extra shirts to be safe." It was signed Marcus and he left his number.

I smiled.

Best Day Ever!

About Dalia Lance

So here is something about little ole me; I have had a very interesting upbringing starting with growing up in Hollywood, CA. Never shy, I learned that if you are not willing to try something new, you may let life simply pass you by. I love meeting people from all walks of life and these experiences inspire me on a daily basis. As a true friend once pointed out "You are never a complete waste, you can always be used as a bad example". So what's the worst that can happen?

Connect with Dalia:
www.DaliaLance.com
Facebook.com/authordalialance
Twitter.com/dalialance
Tumblr: WhoreTips

Other books by Dalia Lance
My Home on Whore Island (Book 1 of the Randi Michaels Novels)
Behind the Veil (Anthology)
The Death of Jimmy (Anthology)

The Terrible Things

By Désirée Matlock

The brakes on the yellow school bus protested as the bus slowed to its last stop at the corner of Second and Eldridge. Max stepped down from the bus slowly, one step at a time. He was met by his big sister Pella, who smiled widely when she saw him. He was glad she was in a good mood, it had been a while.

She turned in the direction of home, but he stayed. He waited for the bus to leave. He didn't want Jim, the bus driver who gave him special attention because of the leg, to see him walk the wrong direction. He didn't particularly like special attention.

"Your mom coming, kid?" Jim was near the end of his route and tired. He usually waited for the kid's mom to walk the seven houses to the stop and get Max. He leaned toward the open bus door and squinted out.

Pella turned to look at the driver. "He's fine."

"It's a short walk to my house." Max didn't mention that he didn't plan to head that direction.

"Can you manage it?" Jim's eyes got even more scrunched as he shifted his squint over to Max's leg.

"I'll be fine. It's a beautiful day out," Max replied. He shifted his weight, adjusting his prosthetic, uncomfortable with the attention.

"I'm here to walk him home," Pella said.

Jim nodded, the bus door already squeaking closed. The brakes huffed indignantly and the bus left to slumber for the night. Max watched as it continued up the hill, all the way to the horizon, and then slipped over it. Max and Pella began walking slowly in the direction of the house together.

Max reached the bush by the big blue mailbox, and he got onto his knees and climbed into the greenery headfirst.

"Max! What are you up to? Get out of that bush."

"I need my board." Max looked up at her, thoughtfully.

"Pella?"

"Yes, pigeon poop?"

"If someone did something bad to me, I mean really bad, what would you do?"

"I'd kill 'em. Duh."

He nodded. "Yeah, me too."

Pella looked down at him quizzically. "Why the weird question? Come on out of that bush. Mom's waiting. And why did you leave your board here?"

"I didn't want to bring it to school today. No she's not. She's visiting grandma." Max didn't want to explain that he had another reason. A reason that wouldn't make any sense. He had a weird sense in the back of his head, that he just needed to do this, that it was time. A sense of real urgency.

He pulled his skateboard out of the middle of the bush, tucked it wheels inward against his ribs, and started to head back out of the bush. His sleeve snagged and Pella reached over, freeing him from the branch. Now on all fours on the sidewalk, he started to get back up. Pella automatically reached out to help him up and he waved her hand away.

"Okay, dad then. Dad's waiting."

"Nope. He went with mom. Remember? We're on our own for a few days. Josh's mom is watching us."

"Huh. Well, I want to get home."

"Why? Why do you want to go home?"

"I don't know. I just really do."

"Well, I want to walk the other direction on Eldridge."

Yes, Eldridge Street. Hurry. It felt like someone was pushing him, mentally, to do this.

"Really? You've had a long day, I'm sure. And you don't look comfortable."

"I am perfectly comfortable with walking the wrong way."

"That's not what I meant," she huffed at him, crossing her arms in front of herself. "I meant-"

"I think you meant that you are uncomfortable with walking that way." He pointed.

"Come on," she said, shoulders rising, "Why would I care?"

"You just do. You don't remember?"

"Remember what?" she said, looking at him with a smile that had lost its happy.

"It's okay, Pella. Come with me if you want, but I'm going and you can't stop me."

Her hands came up. "I just want to know why you want to wander off the wrong way toward the wrong road instead of going home. And," a finger pointed toward him, "I want to make sure you don't get too tired."

"I'm fine." Max sighed. He wasn't weak. "But I need to do something. I can skate if I get tired."

She looked at him doubtfully. "Yeah, right." She knew the board wiped him out harder than anything else.

Max turned around and started walking the other direction. Pella looked at him for a moment, distressed, and then turned to follow.

"Thanks," Max said quietly.

Good idea, bring her to the house. He felt like the thought came without trying.

"Like I could have stopped you." She smiled a big, toothy grin at him and added, "Butthead." He looked up at the sister he loved more than anything in the world, and smiled softly at her. He wanted to hug her sometimes, but was afraid of how it would look.

"Max?"

"Yeah, skittle hog?"

"Psssh. Whatever," she laughed and continued, "Why did mom and dad leave?"

"They needed some space, they said. To get over things. I don't know why they didn't bring me." He shrugged.

"Well, they didn't bring me either. I guess I'm supposed to babysit you. Um, thanks for telling me, guys." She rolled her eyes at their absent parents.

"Yeah, I guess I understand. They were really down after."

"After what?"

"You don't remember? Really?" He paused and shifted the leg on the spot. His leg hurt, but it hurt a lot lately and he didn't want to care about that right now. He stomped the foot hard and twisted slightly to reposition his prosthesis.

"Remember what, kiddo?"

"I kind of figured you were pretending the whole time. So they'd stop asking you stuff."

She looked at him strangely. "You keep talking creepy. Are you okay?"

"Huh. Yeah." He kept walking. The strange gaps in her memory were just part of it, the largest gap being the incident itself. He hoped that what he was planning was a good idea, and wouldn't make things worse.

They walked past the Petersons, past Josh's parents house, past the weird guy with the parakeets. They walked far enough that they were getting into an area where they didn't know so many people.

"Pella?"

"What is it, Stinky?"

He laughed and stuck out his tongue. "Nu-uh, I smell like a flower." He lifted his chin in mock pride.

She snorted. "So, what?"

Max thought for a second and started into the explanation he'd been planning in his head, as to why he personally thought this was important to do, so she'd remember later, when it got hard for her. "Do you remember when we were little and you kept that bully from hurting me?"

"At the park or at the diner?" Her arms swung at her sides again, as she settled into walking beside him.

"Well, either. Do you remember how you kept them from hitting me, and then took care of me?"

"Well, yeah, of course. Some idiot fucker makes my little brother hurt, I'm gonna make him pay." Fucker was her new favorite word, and at fourteen, she could get away with it more than he could. He hadn't tried yet, but hearing her say it made him a little jealous.

"Haha, yeah. You did. But... Well, imagine you're the little sister and I'm the big brother. Would you want me to defend you if someone was hurting you?"

"Well, yeah, I guess..." Sometimes, despite everything, he felt like she was thinking, what could he really do, with a bum leg?

He couldn't remember the hit and run that had taken his leg. He had been too little when the drunk driver hit them. He had been told the story a few times, so he theoretically knew what happened. A gray sedan, possibly a Taurus, had come barreling through a red light, weaving and drunk on a Sunday morning. Smacked into them hard enough to cave in the side of their car, and then kept right on going. Dad and Pella had walked it off, and his mom got a broken rib and a fractured clavicle, but she healed. Max had ended up needing several surgeries before the doctors had insisted on amputating below the knee.

Pella had taken over caring for Max while Mom was in the hospital, and never got back out of the habit. But when he started school at five, Pella wasn't there, and the other kids were mean. He'd moped about it for a little while. His dad had seen what was happening and took him outside to the smoking porch. Dad asked Max like he was a grown up to sit down across from him, and the older man sat puffing away at his Pall Malls for a minute while Max swung his legs. Then Dad had started talking, and Max had paid attention.

Listen, his Dad had said, those kids weren't the problem, Max was. You can't have a problem unless you want it. Listen, he'd said again, the world was always going to have assholes in it, and people were always going to put him in a box. A box called 'weak, incomplete and incapable', and then they'd shoved that box inside another box called 'scary and different'. But those boxes didn't mean jack. Only God and Max knew what he was able to do in life. Maybe God might even send Max a way to make the world better with his bum leg, his dad had said, then added something that really stuck with him, while stubbing out the cigarette.

"Kiddo, you want to change something, change it."

Max had decided. No boxes. The next day, he'd asked for a skateboard. Surprisingly, his dad had said okay. Mom's eyebrows had shot off her forehead, but she'd gone along with it.

In the five years since then, Max had been on his board constantly. He was steadier and lighter and faster on that board than nearly anybody with two legs. The tricks let him fly. The half pipe was a break from the hate. No one at the skate park cared about his leg, they cared about how well he could ollie. It made Mom anxious, but Dad knew. Pella understood, but worried. The skateboard was his armor against the boxes.

Bring her, that's what will make it right.

He hugged his board against himself a little tighter and quickened his step.

"This seems like a long way to go," Pella said.

"We're almost there." He rounded the corner and could see where they were going. They were eight and a half blocks from home now, nearing the brown house with the tan shutters. When Pella saw it, her step slowed.

Come, bring her. This will make it right. He felt the tingle as the thought entered his head without his bidding. It wasn't unfriendly, but it made him uncomfortable.

"No," she said, eyes darting around. "No. I don't like this. Let's go home."

"Look, Pella, I need to do something for you, just like you did with the bullies. Remember how you told me to handle what they said?" She stopped walking, arms crossing in front of her chest again. Max continued anyway, "You told me to repeat the words if I needed, really look at them, and it would make it easier to see what was truth? Well, I think you should do the same thing. And, I have a plan, an idea of what to do, and I need you with me because you're the only one who knows the geography of the place. Like, the layout. I don't know it."

Don't let her stop now. Bring her here, bring her to us. He realized the voice, the urgency, was coming from outside himself, there was no way to deny it anymore. Now that he could see the house, it buzzed at him, and the words came sharper and clearer. He thought for a moment, and agreed with the voices. It definitely had to be done.

"I want to go home. Now." Pella started walking back, still a house away from the brown house with the tan shutters. A picture flashed in front of her eyes of the house in the dark. Of a driveway, a door, of holding on to the door frame with both hands, trying to scream and not being able to. Feeling like she couldn't breath.

"Please, Pella. Please. I can't do this without you."

She started crying, and wandered off the sidewalk to the clean row of trees that lined the road. She leaned against the bark and slid down to the ground. "Oh, damn. I hate crying," she said.

He sat down next to her and tears welled in his eyes. He'd intended to be impervious to emotion, but couldn't help it. "Me, too."

A strange car pulled up, a blue sedan. A frizzy haired woman leaned out the window.

"You okay over there? Hey, aren't you that-"

"Fine!" he said, a little too sharply. Was she too eager? She didn't pull away from the curb, instead she looked at him oddly. Tears from a boy weren't that common, maybe that was why. He waved her off and she reluctantly drove away. He memorized the plate out of habit as it passed him, but then texted it to himself to make sure.

"Why the hell am I crying?" she said.

"Because that house scares you," he said plainly. "It scares me too, but I need to do something. And I need to do it now, while mom and dad are gone. And before Josh's parents show up to watch us. They don't get home until seven, which gives us three hours. To fix this. You, and me. We can do this."

"Do what?"

"Do you remember yet...what happened?"

"No. Do I want to?"

Yes. Absolutely. Pella has to remember. The voice in his head seemed friendly, unthreatening. He somehow wasn't afraid of it, and didn't quite know why. Even though he hoped she wouldn't have to remember to help him.

"Crap. I don't know. It's not going to be fun, but it's got to be better to look at it than forget it."

She stood up. "Okay," she said weakly. "What do I need to do?"

"Just tell me where to go. And maybe be lookout, depending on the place. I don't need you to remember everything, but I need you to remember that house. Just the house. Not what happened in it. Can you do that?"

She has to remember everything. She needs to know everything.

Pella closed her eyes, and thought hard. "No. I can't remember that house. But I remember it anyway. So weird. Looking at it feels like déjà vu. Like I know the house from another life. Seeing the front door, I can remember what the other side of it looks like, they painted it pink but it's all scratched up. And I know that the backyard has one of those stupid fake wells in it."

"I hate those. I mean, what's with no water in a well?"

She snorted through the tears. "I know, right?"

The waterworks slowed down as she kept talking. She pointed. "See there? Those pretty puffy flower bushes under the windows there? I remember seeing them from underneath, from the sticks and ugly side, all tangled and dark, and not from the street. Not from the bright bushy happy part. How do I remember that?"

"I don't know, but I'm guessing you could remember more. But I'm going to ask you stuff you won't want to remember."

No! She must remember everything.

He willed the voices quieter and answered for the first time. Only if she wants to. Only if she wants to remember.

But she has to. There is no other way.

Yes, there is. He thought of his plan, and the house grew quieter.

"Okay, I'll try." She nodded, her too big eyes looking suddenly younger than him. He'd never seen her look so much like a little child. At least she'd stopped crying.

"Do you know where he kept you? Where his things are?"

"No. Who? What things?" She looked a little alarmed and her breathing sped up.

"Okay. It's okay. Don't worry. Maybe you need to see the inside."

"But, whoever lives there might see us. Might get mad at us for going in their house."

"Nobody home. He's not home until Monday. But I'm going to do this, and I'm going in there blind, or you're helping me. Which one?"

"I'm going with you," she said immediately, and started trembling. She took a deep breath and started walking closer.

"Thanks. Okay then." He walked quickly to the house, his leg making a dull ache with each step now. He needed to rest. The operation to remove a new bone spur was still three weeks away, and he wasn't telling anyone how much pain he was in. Enough crap to handle without them taking away the skating.

She trailed just behind him as he stepped onto the walkway to the porch steps.

"No, this way," she said, sticking to the driveway. She walked tentatively down the side of the house, and then hesitated nervously as she approached the back yard.

"Are you sure no one's home?" She looked over her shoulder.

"Yup. Totally positive." Monday, the bad man was going to be released. They'd found out last night, over the phone. Max remembered the call, the prosecutor warning his parents that the charges were going to be dropped on Monday. Something about not enough evidence. Apparently the evidence that had been gathered on the day was useless. His parents had been hugging and crying, and then started packing a bag to head out of town. As if they were in this alone, as if he and Pella hadn't also needed a little breathing room. They hadn't thought about their children at all, but Max's only thought had been of Pella, upstairs in her room, oblivious to the story unfolding around her.

Max had thought about what she'd been through at the hospital, the only part of her ordeal he had been there for. He'd thought about how he'd watched as she'd stared sightlessly up at the green ceiling while her parents held onto each other on the other side of the wall, reporters crowding around the outside doors like crows around roadkill. All kinds of people dressed as blue marshmallows had walked in and out, but he wasn't allowed in. For Max, a soft small sense of desperation had set in then. His dad had cried, and left to go find a place to have a smoke in peace. His mom had developed the sad face she'd worn ever since. As impossible as it seemed, he'd decided he'd help Pella make the bad man pay.

It had been so painful and undignified, after the fact. She should have been wrapped in white pillows and sung sweet music to, instead of being shuffled around a big callous hospital. Sure, treat him like that, he was used to hospitals, but not Pella. Not her. But even after all that, after the scraping, and the wiping and the rubbing of bruises, after white coats carefully sticking Q-tips in little plastic vials, apparently the courier had accidentally destroyed the chain of evidence during delivery.

His folks hadn't tried to pass along the news. He figured that like most things, they didn't think he'd understood. He had, too well. Pella wasn't able to testify, and the physical evidence wasn't going to help anymore. Which left Max.

"He doesn't get home until Monday," he told her. "We have plenty of time."

"Okay. What if someone else comes by?"

"I don't know. But this is when I'm going."

Over here. We're over here. Bring her. The buzz wasn't coming from the house, but the middle of the yard. He suddenly grew scared of being dragged down into the ground, but he still couldn't find anything in the voices that felt dangerous. Like a friend calling to you, it felt right to answer.

"Okay," she said. He wondered if she heard the voices, too, but didn't know how to ask her. She breathed in deep, and started moving toward the thing that scared her.

"Don't touch anything."

"What?" She turned to him, brow furrowed.

"Don't touch anything, unless you touched it last time." He'd seen the crime shows.

Pella raised an eyebrow, nodded once, and walked past the scary part of the yard, right up to the well. She rummaged on the ground for a stick, and then leaned over into the inside. He walked over to see what she was doing. Carefully, with the stick, she was digging a key out from between two bricks. It was a big heavy key he could see, black metal, grunged up and rusty on one side.

She grabbed it as soon as it fell out, and ran over closer to where the voices spoke from, to a cactus thicket in the yard, and carefully rounded behind it.

"Don't get scraped," she said, taking charge. "You be careful." She plunged the key into the ground, and he realized there was a small rectangular door, of muddy exposed wood. It made sense to Max that the police wouldn't have found this very well hidden spot. He put his board down behind a cactus, and pulled a piece of tape from under the wheels to remove a small vial in a plastic baggie that he'd stowed there. He hoped the bright colors of his board couldn't be seen, in case someone came home.

She hadn't noticed what he had done, looking only at the door. She looked around her, then grabbed at the hem of her shirt and used it to open the door up. It swung open and settled against the ground. He looked inside. He could see a few steps downward, toward the house, toward the direction of the urgency, then darkness. He started to walk toward the mouth in the ground.

"Wait! she said, and pointed. There was a tripwire, a thin filament he could barely see, above the second of the steep stairs. She stood still for a second, and then said, "Okay. Let's go, but don't touch that either."

Pella went first, which surprised him. He'd thought it would be harder to get her to go, but now she was leading him down the stairs. He carefully worked his way onto the top step. She quickly jumped over the wire, straight from the first to the third, and then reached toward him to help him down. He didn't take her hand and managed it clumsily, almost not getting his leg over the wire, but couldn't quite skip a step.

At the bottom, his eyes adjusted enough to see that there was no flashlight or lantern nearby. No lightswitch. Nothing. Just a hallway.

"Okay, that's done. Now, let me think. I know the light was on before..." She walked into the darkness.

"Pella, I can't follow you." A few seconds of silence and his heart jumped into his throat. "Pel?" Mom always called him her little grown up, but he couldn't follow her.

He was scared of the voices, sure, but he was also scared of touching something he shouldn't and screwing up the plan.

"It's okay, I'm finding the light switch." Her voice came,

disconnected, out from the dark. Suddenly, bright light flooded the hallway in front of him and he hurried down it, toward the sound of her voice. He walked into a room that felt like it was directly under the scary spot in the yard and saw her there, her shirt pulled off to use as a glove on the light switch that hung almost out of reach on a support pole. She tucked her shirt under her arm.

Good brother. You brought her back to us. We need her. Good brother. We will help her now.

He looked around as the room came into focus. "Oh, my God," he said, without meaning to, as a prayer for strength. The purpose of the room was instantly clear. A beautiful bed with brass headboard and footboard, with glossy, ridiculously shiny golden sheets on it, and a silver comforter, sat dead center in the room. Otherwise it was a drab, simple place, a smooth cube of cement except for the door he'd walked in, and a small metal door halfway up the wall to his left.

Do it. Remember. The voices were calling out now. Remember. Do it. A constant buzz. He could almost hear a few distinct voices, young and innocent. Like children. Like people he would be friends with. He didn't know if she could hear it, but Pella was standing in one spot, turning to look at each thing, a quizzical look on her face. The deja vu again.

He walked over to the wall to his right and looked at the tools that were lined up on it, the kind that could be in anyone's garage. A hammer, a blowtorch, a vise, a few saws, and some he didn't recognize. But in here, near that bed, they spoke to him of terrible things. Of hurting. Of death. How someone could be titillated, how they could get any kind of joy out of harming someone with these things, he couldn't wrap his thoughts around. He shook his head, clearing it of the fear that had bubbled up. Fear of the insidious strangeness of other people thoughts. It wasn't useful right now.

"Turn it off." Pella's voice came small and shaking from behind him. He turned to see that she was seated on the floor, rocking herself. "Turn it off again."

"What?" He went to her as fast as he could. "Turn what off? The light?"

"Turn it off."

Maybe she meant the voices, maybe she meant the light. But it was too late to turn back now.

"I can't do that, Pel. I need you to be strong. You need you to be strong."

She shivered from head to toe and rocked on the spot, her training bra digging into her back as she hunched, the voices chiming away in his head, probably in hers, too. "Let's just do this."

Remember. Remember. Flashes of terrible things happening seemed to whiz past his head. Remember. The voices were getting quieter. Not meant for him, the voices were talking only to Pella now.

He sat awkwardly on the floor, then leaned toward her. She had closed her eyes hard, and silent tears ran toward the floor. Max hated having to, but he whispered, "Tell me what he used when you were here. Tell me, so I can make it better. Or at least better-er."

Tight-lipped, she gripped his arm with one hand, knuckles white. She trembled as she pointed up at a table he hadn't noticed in the corner. From underneath, it was just a rough plywood table, like any table in any woodshop.

He stood and walked over, scared to see what had been used on his sister. Pella, the sister that had taught him to hold hands crossing the street, to not talk to strangers. The sister that had aced her chem test two months before, and then gone missing for six hours only to come home naked and glassy eyed, bleeding from scary places. Ranting, about this house, about the bad man. The sister that had been rushed to the hospital, losing more blood than it seemed like she could hold. The sister who had come home after, blank like a slate. While others roared, she'd become like the empty journals that she was given to write down her feelings, her memories.

Remember. The thought was back to feeling like a gut instinct, faint and distant, and he could no longer hear distinct voices at all. He knew he was no longer in the conversation, and that Pella fought her own demons now.

Max looked down at the table and wondered where to

start.

"It wouldn't help," she said, freeing him from the thoughts that wouldn't stop rolling around in his head. He turned.

"What do you mean?" he said quietly. Everything held still. Was something wrong with the plan? Please let her not tell him something that destroyed the plan. He hadn't seen a hole, but maybe she saw one now.

"It wouldn't help. The rape kit. It wouldn't help because he was careful to only use those things." She pointed, her hand staying pointed as she got up off the floor slowly. He turned back toward the table. He started crying again as he looked down at the terrible things he saw. Things no one should ever have to see. This was a murder room, and he thanked God his sister had escaped. The tears came, and he needed to see what he was doing if the plan was going to work. He took a deep breath to steady himself, wiped his face off on his sleeve and thought again about where to start.

Too many things. He hadn't brought enough. He hadn't planned for this much. A wave of nausea hit him as he tried to keep himself from thinking about what he was looking at.

He tasted bile, but pulled himself together and made himself adjust. He'd only put the stuff onto the things closest to the front of the table. That probably meant that they were the most used, like any other table. Like any other cluttered table. That was how to look at this, objectively, look at it all in line with his plan. He pulled a small dustproof chamois from his front pocket and held it between his fingers. He carefully picked up one of the darkly glistening black items closest to him, but the voices spoke to him suddenly.

No, this one's his favorite. He used it most.

His attention was drawn to a vile black shiny thing at the center of the table, farthest from any edge. He ever so carefully put down what he was holding with the cloth and, table biting into his leg, slowly reached to lift the one the voices said.

Yes, that one. The buzzing in his head almost hurt, but he trusted it. He knew who they were now. He remembered one small flash he'd seen before the voices had started talking mostly to Pella, of real people, with real lives, whose memories had flown past him toward Pella. The memories from behind the tiny metal door, heat rising and smothering, ending the pain, ending everything. He felt a strength rise in him, to do what he'd planned. It wasn't just about him and his sister now.

He was careful to only touch the tiniest bit of the middle part, not the handle that the devil had wielded, nor the end that had hurt so many. He laid it down right in front of him, and studied the handle, working out exactly where the fingers would go when the monster held it.

Good. Do it.

He placed the vial from his hand onto the table next to the terrible thing. Taking another deep breath, he unscrewed the cap, then carefully poured a little of the brown sticky liquid onto the chamois in his hand, folding it away so none would touch his skin.

He started to reach toward the handle of the item with the chamois when he heard Pella's voice, surprising him. "Wait."

He froze, hand suspended, brown liquid almost touching.

She was looking at the table like she'd never seen these things, either. Looking at it with pain in her eyes, but soaking up everything she saw. Tears rolled down her face anew. "Shit," she said. She squared her shoulders. "Fucker. What is that?" she asked.

"I don't know, but he hurt you with it, he hurt all of you with it. So it's what I'm going to hurt him with."

"No, I mean, what is that brown stuff?"

"Oh. I took all of dad's cigarette butts, like a month's worth, and boiled them down into this goop. You can't touch it. It's basically cigarette concentrate. When he touches it, it'll kill him with, like, a heart attack or something. I read about it on the internet a long time ago."

"You remember everything," she said quietly.

"Yeah. Sorry."

"Dad would like that. Dad would like knowing he'd hurt the man," she said, nodding slightly, distantly. Her eyes got thoughtful. "Don't do it yet."

She walked around the room for a minute, touching things. She looked over at him. "Don't worry, Max, I'm not touching new things." She looked so sad, he wished he could take it back. He wished he had walked toward their house instead of turning this direction, toward this house.

She spun back toward the table, walked over and touched a few things. "He did some awful things, Max. To me." One hand rose to her neck, as if she was surprised, while the other delicately touched something sharp. She looked distant, a little disgusted.

"You remember now?" Max asked. It made him queasy again to think about, but he held it together for her.

"Yes. I didn't want to, but now I do." She continued looking around the room, seeming a little more present. "I remember everything. I remember more than everything." She looked at the metal door, and he realized she heard the voices too.

"Do you want me to tell you about what happened?" she asked.

He thought for a second. "If you need to say it out loud, do it. It might help." He took a sharp breath and readied himself.

They stayed there, looking at each other for a minute, and she grew very quiet and calm. To him, she seemed to come into clearer focus as he waited. She didn't look like a little girl anymore. It almost startled him when she started speaking again. "No, I know what the truth is. I don't think I need to tell you, Max. I don't think he should be in both of our heads."

"I'm sorry," Max said really quietly, almost under his breath. "I didn't want to hurt you. I just needed you to tell me where to go. I'm so sorry."

"No, I needed to remember. I needed this visit. Thank you."

Remembered, finally. Thank you, brother.

"Sure, but I don't know. I don't like hurting you."

"You didn't, he did. He's an awful man."

"Okay, well, let me do this," he said as he gestured with the simple cloth laced with death. "Let me hurt him back."

"No. I can do it."

He thought for a second, reluctant. "Okay, if you want to." He offered the poison chamois to her.

She took it extremely carefully, and held it away from her body. "No, I meant that I can talk about it. I can tell them about him. The police. About what Jack did." She pursed her lips and swallowed, staring at the cloth in her hand, and he knew the voices wanted her to do it. She swallowed hard again, her eyes looking more focused.

"I can get him put away where he can't hurt anyone." She wasn't talking to Max now.

The buzzing of the voices, who knew how many, slowed down, thoughtful. Max knew that they all wondered whether being in jail was enough for him.

Max needed to worry about Pella first, and about how hard it would be for her. "Do you want to do that? You'd have to really want to, because that's telling a bunch of strangers what happened." And it might not work, Max added to himself. "Can you do that?"

Her eyes gleamed with purpose. "I can. I will. I'll even lead them here. Look, I don't want you to become a killer like the bad man. Like Jack." She walked over to the bed and touched the curly metal with one finger, staring at it oddly. "You don't want you to be like him, Max. You know that."

She stood at the head of the bed she'd been held in, staring down its length, and then spat on a pillow.

"Yes, I understand." His eyes got hard. "But if he gets away with it, I'm coming back."

"Of course."

"I'll help if you need it. But we only have until Monday, or he gets released."

"Right," she said. She carefully pulled her shirt back on and wiped the hair away from her face with her free hand. "Let's go, then. You didn't touch anything did you? We don't need to confuse the cops when they get here."

He shook his head. He'd been careful – no hands. He closed and bagged up the vial, zipped it into the baggie tightly, then rolled into his pocket.

The voices were buzzing with uncertainty. They hadn't decided whether jail or death was the best way, and he wanted to leave before they did.

Pella must have felt the same way, because she moved to the light switch. "All right, fart breath, go climb out of this hell hole, and I'll race you to the police station - you skate, I'll run," she instructed him, sounding like her old self again, bossy and strong, but different. At the door, looking back at her for a second, she shone to him, standing by the light switch. He walked back out the hallway toward the sunshine, then started pulling himself up to the outside. It took a little while for him to clear the trip wire, then the top step, but she kept the light on for him.

"Okay, I'm out!" he called as loudly as he could without neighbors hearing, then went over to the skateboard and picked it up, pain forgotten. He turned around, waiting for Pella.

"Okay, here goes," she said, mostly to herself, as the room went black.

About Désirée Matlock

Désirée Matlock presently lives in a beach town with her beau, twin daughters, two cats and a dog, where, whenever she gets two seconds to rub together, she writes by a window overlooking a lake. She loves to travel and play the piano, although never at the same time. She won't bore you further with the mundane details of her simple life unless you visit her blog.

Connect with Désirée online:
www.DesisTwoCents.com

Other books by Désirée Matlock
On the Verge (Anthology)
Into the Abyss (Anthology)

Final Gift

By Anne Cargile

Gabriel had every contour of her body etched into his mind. He had drawn every muscle, in every angle she could make. He knew every hair on her body, every freckle, like he knew his own. Clara was lovely, but what had made her perfect as a subject had been her innocence, her jejune.

He hadn't found any challenge in seducing her. The challenge had been in keeping the deception going. He knew if he were to go to her now, go in there and tell her that everything was all right, she would forgive him. She'd crawl to him and kiss his feet. She'd be grateful and happy.

Gabriel sighed, knowing that he had reached the end of inspiration with a subject. He had no more sketches to do, no more paintings. He wished he could do more, but really, it was out of his hands. Clara had been his muse, for a while, and now she had only one more thing to give to him.

It had taken him years of experimentation to develop the method for his sculptures. So much time, so many failures. Those had been heartbreaking. Gabriel had almost given up his vision. Starting with small pieces at first, he had gradually been able to achieve pieces on a scale that satisfied him artistically.

Thankfully, what he was about to do was something he only had to do once per subject. It was incredibly time-consuming, and risky. He'd thrown away entire bodies of work devoted to one subject when this, the final step, had failed him. Gabriel hated waste.

Looking at the calculations on his desk, he glanced at the computer monitor to see how Clara was coping with her new surroundings. He had chloroformed her earlier and placed her in the special tank, arranging her body to his satisfaction while she had been unconscious. Now she should be waking up, and he hoped he could begin soon. She needed to be fully awake for the piece to achieve the level of intensity required. Gabriel saw her moving her head, her eyes blinking open.

He would need to go in soon, but not yet and he turned to focus on the computer program; no errors could be made in this final step. He gathered himself together, and finished entering the calculations that would start the pumping process into the chamber. The chemicals had to be delivered in exactly the correct quantities, at exactly the right times to ensure adhesion.

Finished, Gabriel stood and stretched. Walking out of the small room that served as his office he went down the short hall and passed through a thick door at the end. Entering the room that held Clara, Gabriel walked over to several tanks against the wall and started flipping switches on the control panel. He knew Clara could see him, but she was well trained now and wouldn't speak unless spoken to first.

"Clara, darling," Gabriel called out. He could feel her attention riveted on his voice. "I want to thank you. You have been my inspiration and my muse. For the last eight months that you have given me, I will give you immortality." He paused. "Everything ends. It's time to say goodbye Clara. I'm sorry I can't kiss you, I cannot stroke you. I won't be able to see your eyes. But I will be here, with you through every moment of your transcendence. Goodbye Clara." His voice was gentle.

He walked over to the tank and saw the confusion on Clara's face. She was naked and kneeling in the small tank, her skin glistening with perspiration. The tank looked somewhat like a very large fish tank, with thick Plexiglas walls, completely sealed except for the tubes that would pump in the chemical compounds.

He gave her a final assessing look, checking one last time that everything was as perfect as he could make it. Her arms were fixed in a position of supplication or prayer, slightly elevated above her head. He had done her hair, but was doubtful about it lasting through the process. Her face clean of make-up, she was as perfect as he could ask.

Gabriel blew her a kiss through the glass and walked out of the room, firmly shutting the door behind him. Besides having the benefit of sealing the environment in the room, it cut off all sound.

Walking back into his office he sat at his desk and pulled his keyboard to him. He would be able to watch the events on his monitor, and see what Clara would gift him with.

"Goodbye sweetheart," he whispered, and pushed Enter on his keyboard.

The nitrogen started pumping from the tanks, and Gabriel saw when it first hit Clara's body. He couldn't hear her, but her mouth opened in a scream of terror. Her body started to convulse in the small tank, thrashing violently. The nitrogen was in liquid form, spraying her from several angles, so there was really no escape. Gabriel thought he had fixed her position securely enough, but her movements were much more violent than he had expected. He chewed his lip, worried she might break free of the form he had set and ruin everything.

With the cold passion of a scientist Gabriel noted Clara's mouth opening to an almost impossible width. It was fascinating to watch a subject's animalistic reactions. When Clara swung her head around, screaming, she got a spray of liquid nitrogen full blast to her face. He could see her choking. As the liquid filled the small tank Clara's movements quickly slowed. Her body began to freeze into position. Gabriel blew a sigh of relief. His design would hold.

The liquid had passed the level of her stomach, and he saw Clara's movement stop. She was nearly gone. At -196 degrees, the liquid nitrogen was causing almost instant freeze. Gabriel sat at his desk and watched his beautiful Clara die.

But she'll live forever because of me, he thought, giving her death the solemnity it deserved.

He watched while the tank completed filling. Checking his computer, he saw it would be at least twelve hours before the freezing process was complete enough for him to initiate the next system. He would go grab something to eat, clean up his studio maybe. He had a lot to do before he could take a well-deserved vacation.

He left his office and walked outside, whistling.

***

Gabriel watched the gathering in silence. He leaned against a wall, and the wind blew his hair over his face, concealing his eyes. He knew they were there for him, to see what he had done. He wasn't sure why he cared, or even if he did, but he stood on the sidewalk anyway, behind the shadow of the streetlamp, smoking, watching. *There they go, pampered, powdered and perfumed, like any of it mattered*, he thought.

He took a final drag from his cigarette and threw it in the street as he walked towards the gallery entrance. Time to see Clara again.

Several months had passed since he had delivered his paintings and the final sculpture to his art dealer in New York. He had hied himself off to his boat in the Caribbean for a well-deserved vacation immediately after he'd received confirmation of delivery. Gabriel always came back for his opening nights though. He knew he shouldn't care, but he was compelled to see his muses one last time before they went off to a new master. He had been especially fond of Clara, and felt he owed her this farewell.

He walked briskly up the steps to the gallery and presented his invitation to the tuxedoed doorman, pleased with the turnout he saw inside. He passed through the doors quickly, noticing the flower arrangements tastefully placed in alcoves and on tables. Good, he thought, they had followed his instructions to the letter. He always chose a different flower for his opening night, in memory of his muse. This one was the lily. White ones, for Clara's innocence.

Grabbing a glass of whiskey from a passing waiter, Gabriel meandered through the throng, listening in on the gossip. Very few people would have recognized him, as he never announced himself at these openings. He preferred to stay in the background, the better to enjoy the titillating responses from the attendees.

Gabriel saw his agent, and raised his glass of whiskey in a mock toast, grinning. His agent was a very wealthy man because of Gabriel Marks, and knew it.

His agent's name was Mr. Whiting; a simple name for a man who was far from simple. One of the best artist's agents in the world, tall and well built, Mr. Whiting, who apparently had no first name, was impervious to the indiscretions of lesser men. He had a baritone voice, and a perfectly snobby Euro accent that screamed class and style. Very few people were able to stand up to the man's polished veneer.

Mr. Whiting was unscrupulous in serving his clients, and that suited Gabriel just fine. As long as his instructions were obeyed in how the shows were arranged, Gabriel could care less what his agent did.

Gabriel was wondering if he had time to run outside for another smoke when he heard the light ringing of a silver bell, calling attention to the curtained area along one wall. The crowd started to mill that way, excitement fizzing the air like champagne bubbles.

The heavy red curtains were drawn back, and the main gallery was revealed. The room was fairly long and wide, gently lit except for spotlights highlighting the art that hung on the walls. The carpet was a deep plush that muffled sound, and at the far end was another red curtain that encircled a wide round platform. There were at least thirty pieces to be viewed before reaching the end of the room, and the crowd was impatient despite their consumption of alcohol. They started to push to be the first to see Gabriel's new work, using an occasional elbow to remove an adversary.

They looked like a herd of cattle, Gabriel thought, laughing to himself. He took his time, stopping occasionally to remember the events in special paintings, in no hurry to get to the final piece on the platform. He stopped at one painting and his breath caught. Naked, and washing her feet in a bowl, Gabriel remembered that Clara had just come in from the garden. She had smelled of fresh dirt and sunshine. He inspected his painting critically and saw the flaws. There. He hadn't caught the luminosity that had shone in her hair. The painting was a failure, and Gabriel moved on to the end of the room, disappointed in his skill.

Fog crawled along the floor near the platform, thanks to a cleverly concealed machine. Silver light glowed from above, shining directly down on the center of the hidden platform, making the dark red curtain look like dried blood. The horizon line where the red of the back lit curtain met the fog created a hellish tableau. Gabriel stopped to observe, and was exceptionally pleased with the effect.

He moved closer but could barely make out the shape behind the curtain. He heard the curious murmurs as people moved to try and get a glimpse of what lay behind.

Mr. Whiting and his assistant came and stood quietly in front of the dais, the light through the curtain washing their skin in the deep crimson hues of dripping blood.

Mr. Whiting stood patiently until the majority of the attendees had gathered in front of him. The silvery light above had grown steadily brighter, and the curtain's glow was now the bright red of a fresh arterial cut. The shadow cast on the spectators made them look as if they had been wallowing in pools of the stuff, and with the shine in their eyes, the gathered art lovers looked like a clowder of maniacal followers. Gabriel had to bite his cheek hard to prevent his laughter from bursting forth. It was perfect.

Mr. Whiting gave his assistant a nod, and she pulled out a small remote control. With gentle ceremony she pushed a button and the curtain started to lift toward the ceiling. The silver light began to wash over the floor, covering the gathering in it's brilliance.

Gabriel felt his eyes tear up. He knew he was the only person in the room who could see Clara as she should be seen. When her light shone down on him, it washed him clean, and he felt her forgiveness. The power of her beauty forced him to his knees. The murmurs of the crowd faded to silence, abruptly and suddenly, as the piece became clear.

Centered in the middle and raised up on the dais, Clara knelt. Impossibly bright, she glowed with an incandescence that lifted Gabriel's soul. Her body was postured in supplication to the light above, her face fixed in her final scream of pain, locked in bronze.

It was the artist's final vision, and Clara's final gift to him.

<<<◇>>>

About Anne Cargile

After decades of trying to ignore the voices in her head and appear normal Anne Cargile finally sat down one day and let them take over. She habitually only shared her mental adventures with her garden plants, but they steadily worked to convince her to share with humans too. She finally gave in to their incessant nagging and has been working on writing and publishing her stories to "real" people. Squeezing in time to tap out a few pages a day between the demands of her family, her chickens and her half acre garden Anne currently resides in New Hampshire.

Connect with Anne online:
facebook.com/Anne-Cargile
Email: Anne.Cargile@gmail.com

Other books by Anne Cargile
The Death of Jimmy (Anthology)
Into the Abyss (Anthology)
Beyond the Threshold (Anthology)

Yellow Ribbons

By Alanna J. Rubin

I arrived at our tree and suddenly feeling nervous, ran a hand through my hair and loosened my cravat which felt too constricting. We had often visited here, fond of the solitude and shelter the branches and leaves offered from the rest of the world. The tree had heard our dreams and woes and was as much a part of our lives as a dear friend. For hours we would sit and I never tired of watching the wind play with her hair. Once, I was offered the magnificent sight of a gust of wind knocking free the yellow ribbon that had meddlesomely prevented her hair from cascading down around her shoulders. I had retrieved it, for it was her favorite ribbon, but I put it in my pocket in protest, refusing to let it once more imprison her curls.

It was here that I felt closest to her and reflexively, I withdrew the ribbon. It had become my constant companion since her passing, a way of keeping her close. I sat at the base of the tree, my back propped up against the trunk, legs bent while rubbing my thumb back and forth across the now worn surface of the ribbon, as I struggled to put my feelings into words.

"My Love...," I started then paused, unsure how to continue, "it began when my friends tried to draw me out of the mire of my thoughts to engage in nights of titillating adventures. The idea was abhorrent. In response, I retreated into a sanctuary created of our belongings. For the past five years I have immersed myself in the memories that we shared, reliving every touch of our hands, the feel of your lips upon mine, every embrace. For so long I have lived among these memories that they have felt more real than the very ground beneath my feet. But as of late, the memories feel less solid as I am drawn back out into the world of the living. With each passing day the world seems brighter, more whole, and full of promise. The only explanation I can offer is *her* — a wisp of a girl that appeared at my doorstep inquiring about work four months ago. Impossible.

Solitude was my only companion aside from you so I turned her away, but inexplicably she showed up the next day offering her skills as a housemaid. Angered by her audacity, I turned her away without a second thought, rid of her, I was sure, once and for all. Until the next day," I chuckled at the remembrance, "but this time confusion took the place of anger when I sent her away. It went on like this for a fortnight. Eventually I found myself looking forward to the encounter, but I turned her away all the same.

"Then something remarkable happened. One day she arrived at my door, and I laughed for the first time since your departure from this world. Any objection I had regarding her employment melted away and she has been my housemaid since. She sings as she carries out her duties scurrying to and fro, bringing so much vigor, so much life into my world. It beams out of her like rays from the sun. Her radiance blinds me, yet I cannot bring myself to look away. I find her light to be a healing balm to a soul I long since thought had withered."

I hesitated, afraid to say what must next be said and I looked to the ribbon for strength. "I need her," I said softly. "The memories in which I lost myself for so long feel as if they are slipping away, taking their rightful place as moments to treasure rather than a world of escape. I cannot help but feel a sense of guilt as if I'm betraying you." I could not go on. Tears of mourning and grief long held in fell for the first time since my beloved left this world.

Was it minutes or hours that had passed while my pent up sorrow was purged from my being? I knew not, but when my tears were spent, the pain and sorrow that had been my constant companions could not be found. I beheld the yellow ribbon laying across my palm. It became a bridge that reached across the chasm between this world and the next, connecting our souls.

"I love you," I whispered. My words were met with a warm breeze that embraced me, then slowly transformed into a gust of wind that swept the ribbon away into the vastness of the sky. I watched it until it disappeared against the brightness of the sun. As the leaves of our tree rustled melodically overhead, instilled within me was a sense of peace and finally, I was able to say, "Goodbye".

As I looked out toward the horizon and saw the faint outline of my estate, what I must do next became clear. I mounted my horse and began to close the distance to my home. When drew near, I was struck by the beauty before me; the green of the grass, the smell of the wild lavender in the air, the vibrant colors of the roses in my garden. It was as if everything had been imbued with new life, but I knew what had changed was me. I was looking upon the world with a newly opened soul, and it was if the world was singing. Energized, I guided my horse to the servants' entrance. It was the best way to ensure that I would not be discovered. I did not wish her to see me, not yet.

Quietly, I made my way up to my rooms and looked around the dark surroundings in which, not long before, I found comfort. Now stifling, I threw open the heavy curtains to let the light of day stream in and christen the room anew. Satisfied, I turned my attention back to the task at hand and located the box of family jewelry that lay neglected on the bottom of my armoire. I drew it out carefully and blew off a thick layer of dust from the lid. My quest would not take long to complete as I knew exactly what I sought. Within moments I found my quarry and withdrew a velvet wrapped box which contained a daintily set sapphire that glistened in the sunlight when I opened the lid. "Perfect," I said as I snapped the lid shut with a satisfying click. I left the room knowing exactly where I would find her and I was not disappointed.

Lovelier than when I had seen her last, she glided to and fro, tinkering with this and that whilst sweetly humming her favorite melody. Silently, I admired her from the doorway. I had desired to make sure every nuance of this moment would be indelible, but her enjoyment caused a laugh to escape my lips. Startled, she turned around abruptly. Upon seeing me, a smile graced her mouth and her eyes sparkled. A light beamed from her very being and it reinvigorated my spirit. My grip tightened around the box in my hand. Certain of my future, I approached the woman who had saved me, the woman whom I loved beyond words could say. Once again, I felt whole.

***

I remembered when I first arrived in town. Near destitute, I took only what was mine when my father sent me away after I refused to marry the oaf of a man he had chosen for me. I went gladly, certain that I would find work as a housemaid, but after the fourth great house sent me away for lack of references, I began to despair. Against my better judgment, I went to the local pub to enquire with the owner if there was any work to be had. Shaking his head no, I gave him a thruppence for a bit of bread and water. I felt uncomfortable surrounded by so many men staring at me in a licentious manner with what was sure to be whiskey in hand. I pulled my cloak tightly around my neck in an effort to ward off the discomfort and ate as slowly as possible. I feared it may be my last for some time.

Pitifully, I was eyeing the last morsel on my plate when I was joined by a woman. Though pretty, she had a face whose features were unremarkable except one—she had a dimple in the middle of her chin. Such a thing was unusual to see, but it lent an added charm to her smile, which exuded a warmth that instantly put me at ease.

She asked, "How is it you came to be in a place such at this?" Although she asked the question, the look in her eye told me she already knew the answer. As I was about to give her my reply, she held up her hand to stay me. "I apologize. It is none of my business. You are clearly in need of work and I know of a situation. Would you like to hear?" I nodded my head excitedly, which was all the encouragement she needed. "There is an estate not far from here that is in desperate need of a housemaid, but the master there is known to be a bit of a recluse. Since the passing of his wife some years ago he has refused anyone seeking employment."

"Then why...," I began.

She finished my question. "Would he hire you?" I nodded. Her tone became serious and her eyes were touched with sadness. "Because he needs *you*. You just have to convince him of it." She squeezed my hand reassuringly, but the touch was startling and my hand tingled even after she let go. It took me a moment to regain my composure and I was about to ask how, when she rose to leave. "Here are the directions to his estate. Remember, you must persevere. He will not be welcoming, but your patience will be rewarded." She left just as mysteriously as she had arrived. I drew the paper with the directions closer to me, ate the last bit of bread on my plate, and started my journey.

Unfamiliar with the geography of the area, it took me a half a day's walk to reach the estate. It was magnificent despite the apparent neglect. I made my way up the drive to the front door, which had lanterns hanging on either side. Taking the heavy cast iron knocker in my hand, I rocked it against the door with a confidence that belied the anxiety I felt. The door was not answered, so I knocked again and again. When the door did finally open, a man appeared. His handsome features were marred with the burden of loss and his eyes held no welcome, but I would not be cowed.

"I'm here to be your housemaid," I announced. His countenance turned from anger to confusion to outrage in the span of a moment and he slammed the door without a word. Clearly he was the master of the house of which the woman spoke. I knocked several more times to no avail and grew frustrated. His poor manners did nothing more than spur me on. It was too late to head back into town, so with my head held high I found his stables and, together with a clowder, made myself comfortable enough to spend the night.

Steeling myself for battle, I returned the next day, but our encounter was again brief, for he slammed the door once more without hesitation. Vexed, I retreated back to his stables and ate berries I had found nearby, which fed me well enough. I, too, was stubborn and would not be dissuaded by his rude behavior, but after several days my resolve weakened and I questioned my being there. An image of the woman rose in my mind, and the sincerity of her plea gave me strength to continue the battle. The next day I knocked on the door again and when he appeared, something had changed behind his eyes. For the first time I saw hope. I felt something tug at the very fiber of my being and it became clear to me that I could never abandon him. After this encounter, no longer did he slam the door directly following my arrival, rather he would look at me as if seeing a friend. Shaking his head, he would exasperatingly say, "please go away," but there was hesitation in his words and movements, as if pleading with me to try again tomorrow as he disappeared behind the heavy wooden door. A routine developed, which I rather looked forward to. Finally, he came to the door and when he saw me he laughed. I was disarmed; his laugh was beautiful and intoxicating. That was the moment I fell in love with him.

From that day I was his housemaid, but he has been more than that to me. He was my home, my love and I was determined to help him overcome the allure of living in the past, and instead embrace the present. Over the months, I encouraged him to leave his rooms for extended periods of time, to take his meals in the dining room, and venture outside. I accompanied him one day to the gardens, but once sure of his well being, I moved to give him space. He reached out and took my hand to keep me by his side. I felt his pulse, at first racing, steady into a beat harmonious with my own.

I had taken to humming a melody that reminded me of him. It quickly became my favorite and hardly a moment passed when its notes were not my companion. I was cleaning the parlor when I heard laughter from behind me. It jarred me from my thoughts and abruptly I turned around. Before me stood a man no longer burdened by sorrow, but whose soul was at peace. The mirth that danced in his eyes drew a smile from me that contained all of the wishes for happiness I possessed. He walked toward me with determination and a glint in his eyes that stirred butterflies in my stomach. Gently he held my hand and took to one knee, presenting me with a small velvet box. Only in my dreams had I dared to hope that he loved me as much as I did him. Now as we embraced, our hearts rejoiced as one. Silently, I gave thanks to the woman I met in town so many months before.

A month later, we were wed. I stood in the foyer of our home surrounded by pictures of his loved ones who looked down upon us smiling, but the one that was of interest most was never present.

"My love," I started and then stopped.

"What is troubling you? Pray tell me," he prodded.

I hesitated. I had never asked to see her portrait, always anxious that it might bring on a melancholy, but that day I felt compelled. "May I see the portrait of your wife?" I asked gently.

He looked at me in confusion, but replied, "Of course. I'll have Bromley bring it down from my rooms. It's time she rejoined the rest of my family in the gallery."

Within minutes, the portrait was brought down. I walked toward it in shock. It was her, the woman from town. I was certain of it. Down to the dimple on her chin, the warmth of her smile, and the yellow ribbon that perfectly adorned her hair.

About Alanna J. Rubin

Writer, Whovian, Jane-ite, Trekkie, & Geek. She could go on, but you get the idea. Originally from Massachusetts, she never missed an opportunity to pick apples, carve pumpkins, or go to Salem for witches and haunted happenings. Now in Florida, not a day goes by when she doesn't miss the changing colors of leaves, but wouldn't give up not having to shovel snow. Often, she finds herself torn between watching a Jane Austen adaptation or hopping on the Tardis for an adventure in time and space.

Connect with Alanna online:
www.AlannaRubin.com
twitter.com/AlannaRubin
facebook.com/AlannaRubin

Molly

By Erika Lance

Paul was sitting at the table in his kitchen staring into his bowl of soggy cereal. He closed his eyes for a moment and thought back to when he would wake up to the smell of an amazing breakfast being prepared. He would come into the kitchen and Ivy would have breakfast ready before he had to run out the door to an important meeting at work. The kind of meeting he had every morning, they didn't seem nearly as important now.

He could see her standing at the sink wearing the pair of shorts and tank top that she liked to sleep in. She would be singing the words of whatever song she said was rolling around in her head. Ivy said that singing it out loud caused it to stop being stuck in her head. Paul was never sure if the logic was sound, but with the beautiful woman in front of him, it didn't have to be.

Ivy had loved musicals. When he would ask her what song she was singing, she would laugh and tell him the name as if he should have remembered it. He *should* have remembered, he thought as he opened his eyes.

Ivy had started dragging him to shows when they were still dating. Paul had gone, knowing that she loved them and that she would go to every sporting event he asked her to without complaint. She even learned what the plays meant, who the teams were and even the names of the players. She had an amazing memory.

He stared into the bowl in front of him and found he had stirred his spoon around enough that it had mushed the soggy flakes into an even more liquefied state. Ivy would not have wanted him to sit there feeling guilty about not knowing the title song to the musical *Chicago*. She would have smiled, told him how adorable he was, and kissed his forehead.

Before he could sink deeper into his guilt his phone

beeped.

It was his secretary reminding him to bring in the Drabrough proposal. He had worked on it for the last two months, and the meeting was that day. Drabrough Manufacturing had been shopping around to decide where to build their largest manufacturing plant to date. Paul had this one opportunity to have them choose the east coast and close the largest deal of his career.

He texted a reply, put his bowl in the sink and headed out. He would stop for coffee on the way in. He hadn't figured out how to use the fancy French press that Ivy had made the most amazing coffee in.

When he began to pull out of garage he spotted a small pink plastic car in the rear facing camera on his dashboard. He put his car in park, opened the door and got out. The pink car belonged to his neighbor's daughter. At four years old she rode the motorized car around as if she was a race car driver. She always had a stuffed dog in the seat next to her.

Paul smiled a little. He and Ivy would sit on the front porch on Saturday mornings, enjoying a cup of coffee and watch her drive up and down the sidewalk. His smile faded and he tried to turn on the car to steer it out of the way. The battery was dead so he pushed it onto his lawn. He knew Marci or Ben would be over to grab it soon enough to get it charged back up.

Paul got back in his car and headed to work. That had been enough memories for one morning. He had heard the cliché that 'time heals all wounds'. He wished someone could tell him the amount of time he would wait to heal his wound. It was deep, and hurt constantly.

~~~

Ivy had died on a Sunday.

Paul had received the call from Barbara, his mother-in-law, on a Friday night. Ivy had started bleeding and been taken by ambulance to Trinity Memorial Hospital in critical condition. Barbara had tried to explain more, but Paul only heard the pulse in his ears as his heart felt like it was going to burst from his chest. He got on the next flight back, a redeye. He had been in California on a 'team building' weekend for his firm.

He arrived at the hospital at 8:47am to find Ivy in ICU. He wasn't allowed in the room. He looked at her lying in the hospital bed and the only thing he recognized was the color of her hair splayed across the pillow where her head rested.

He leaned against the window and tried to will himself into the room. He wanted her to at least know he was there, by her side.

As he looked at all of the tubes and monitors sticking out of the only girl he had ever loved, he heard a voice in his head screaming to not give up, that she would be ok, that they would both be ok. But there was that part of him, the dark part that saw the scene unfolding in front of him, that knew she wasn't going to leave that room.

Paul felt a hand on his shoulder. It was Barbara, his mother-in-law. Her husband Roy was just behind her, standing stoically. Roy was from the generation of men that didn't cry in front of others. Any grief he was feeling, any pain, he would bear alone.

Paul turned and hugged Barbara, pulling her close. She hugged him back, rubbing his back the way one does when comforting a child.

"The doctor will be back soon and needs to speak with you Paul," she said in a whisper.

He pulled back from the embrace and nodded as he let his gaze wander again to Ivy.

The doctor did speak with him. He explained to Paul that Ivy had suffered a miscarriage, which resulted in tremendous blood loss. When the emergency team arrived she had not been responsive.

Paul was confused because Ivy hadn't been pregnant.

Paul felt frozen. He heard the doctor's words, could hear their meaning, but he couldn't make it real. Paul tried to remember the last thing Ivy had said to him and couldn't.

Paul pulled out his phone to look at the last texts he had received from her the night before.

"Wish you were here to bring me ice cream and rub my

feet"

"I love you PBJ"

Ivy had called him PBJ since their first date. What was supposed to be an amazing romantic picnic, they got rained out just as they had set everything up. Ivy invited him over to her place to dry off, and they had made peanut butter and jelly sandwiches and watched JAWS on TV, commercials and all. It had been perfect in the end. She had been perfect.

Now Ivy was lying in a bed in the next room and at the same time, she wasn't. Looking at the person hooked up to the machines Paul felt so many emotions at once he thought he would break. Hope was the worst of them, the small irrational part of him that thought she would open her eyes and she would get better.

He had tried to see her, after Ivy's family had gone in, but he had known he wasn't ready.

The doctor had explained that even though there was no brain activity, Ivy could still experience pain. What had happened to her, what was still happening, was incredibly painful, and although they were feeding her painkillers there was no way to know what she was feeling.

Paul knew it wasn't about what *he* was feeling, but he wanted time to figure out the perfect thing to say, something that would have made Ivy smile while tears streamed down her face. He had been able to do that when he asked her to marry him. He had planned the whole thing for months. He'd had months. Now he only had minutes, minutes to tell the person that meant everything to him goodbye.

As he entered the room he heard the hum and beeping of the machines. He looked at the displays and saw her heartbeat move across the screen. That little voice of hope started to creep in to say that she would and could get up. He sat in the chair next to the bed and picked up her hand. It was warm. He remembered how she would sometimes sneak up behind him when he was working and rub her cold fingertips on this neck. Now, they were warm.

Paul sat and held his wife's hand not knowing how much time passed. He tried to start talking at least ten times, but couldn't get any words to come. He did know how to say that this wasn't supposed to happen; he wasn't ready to lose her. He didn't know how he would live without her, but that moment wasn't about him. It was about her, and he didn't know what to say.

He had been staring at horizon themed wall border when he heard the first alarm go off. He heard motion behind him and he tried to see what was happening. Where was the heartbeat line? A nurse pushed him kindly but firmly away from the bed, saying something about stepping out of the room. He didn't want to let go.

Ivy died at 3:04am.

~~~

Paul got home late. The Drabrough Proposal had been a hit. He had won the bid and his team had gone out to celebrate. It was the largest deal he had ever closed and it meant a promotion. At work he could go through the motions and make things happen. It was when he wasn't at work that he felt alone again.

As he drove up to his house he saw that the pink jeep was still on his lawn. He pulled into the garage and closed it. Grabbing his laptop bag he went into the house, set the bag on the couch and went out the front door. He needed to grab the mail anyhow and he was surprised that the jeep was still there. He got the mail and looked toward the neighbor's house. Their lantern shaped porch light was still on and so was the one in the living room. He could see it through the curtains. Although a little late he didn't think that Marci or Ben would mind if he knocked.

Paul went up to the pink jeep and began to pick it up. It was heavy but he thought he could use the back wheels to roll it across the yard. He found it had been charged up and was able to steer it over, unlike that morning.

A little puzzled Paul knocked on his neighbor's door. Marci answered. "Hi Paul, is everything ok?" she asked. Marci and Ben were in their mid-thirties. Marci was a stay at home mother and blogger, and Ben was an engineer.

"I'm fine. I was just returning..." he said gesturing at the Jeep. "I found it on my lawn and figured it should be inside."

Marci thanked him and called for Ben to come move the Jeep inside their garage. "I am actually glad you stopped by. I have something for you," she said handing him a folded piece of construction paper.

Paul looked at it and heard Marci say, "Molly made it for you. She said to give it to you today."

Paul smiled a little. "Tell her I said thank you."

"I will. If you need anything, Ben and I are here," Marci said.

Paul just nodded. It was what most people had said to him over the last few months.

"Goodnight," he said to both of them as Ben returned from putting up the jeep. He headed back to his house with his mail and the paper.

When he got inside he threw the mail on the kitchen counter and then changed into his p.j. bottoms and a t-shirt. He switched on the TV and went into the kitchen to grab a drink.

He took the cup that had been sitting in the sink, the same one he used every night. He rinsed it, put a few ice cubes and then filled it to the top with whiskey. It had become Paul's ritual. Taking his first swig he shook his head a little. He had become everything they tell you not to when you lose someone.

Dr. Hayes, his therapist, told him it was part of the grieving process, and that as long as he kept working and getting better, not to worry. Paul liked Dr. Hayes. When he couldn't sleep the first week after, he had decided to get some help. His first call had been to get pills that would knock him out. Dr. Hayes would only prescribe them if Paul was willing to see him at least once a week. Paul agreed.

Dr. Hayes had helped. Paul could talk to him when he felt as if there was no one else. Paul knew there were others, his family, her family, and friends. He wasn't ready to share her with them just yet.

He sat in front of the TV and let it take him places. He usually stuck to action and horror movies; anything without titillating sex scenes, romance or musical numbers.

He got up to refill his glass when he noticed the folded piece of paper on the counter. He smiled and opened it. He read it and shook his head. He must be a little drunker then he thought, although one cup was usually only good for a slight buzz now.

It was a picture of a smiling yellow sun with a rainbow behind it and it said: Bee Happpy

He crumpled the paper and threw it in the trash. He didn't know what about it upset him exactly, but he grabbed the bottle off the counter and headed back to forget again.

He woke up to the sound of the alarm going off on his phone, the bottle laying next to him on the couch. His head was pounding. He debated calling in, but after yesterday's win there would be a ton of work to do. If he stayed home it wouldn't end up being rest.

He took a couple of ibuprofen and got into a hot shower. When he was dressed he decided to pick up something on the way in. Paul knew that diving into his job would offer a reprieve, and he spent the next couple of nights at work until the wee hours. He only went home to sleep and change his clothes. He didn't need the bottle those nights, he was exhausted enough when he walked in the door.

It was Friday before he knew it. Wrapping up at work around 11pm, he checked his phone and saw two voicemails. One was from Ivy's mother Barbara, and the other from Dr. Hayes office. The latter he assumed was to confirm his appointment first thing Monday morning. Paul found Mondays had worked best to help him deal with the week. He verified and deleted. He decided to wait until he got home to listen to Barbara's.

As he pulled into his driveway he saw the pink Jeep was again sitting in front of his porch. He looked over but the lights were out next door. He moved the Jeep into his garage so it wouldn't disappear during the night.

When he woke up the next morning the sun was already bright in the sky. He used to hate sleeping in on weekends, it seemed like there was always something to do. Now, it helped eat up time. He checked his phone and saw another voicemail from Barbara. Worried something was wrong, he listened to the most recent   message. Barbara just asked him to call and let them know he was alright, that she hadn't intended on offending him if she had.

He listened to the other message.

Barbara asked Paul if he needed help to pack up Ivy's things, and that she understood he needed time. Ivy would have wanted her clothes donated to help a local charity, and friends and family had asked about a few things that had belonged to Ivy.

Paul called her back while he made a pot of coffee and poured a bowl of cereal.

When she answered he told her he was fine. She didn't ask about the stuff. Barbara was polite like that. She would wait till he said something, so he did. He told her he wasn't ready to go through the stuff just yet, but that he would soon, within the month. Dr. Hayes had said it was better to go through it sooner rather than later. Barbara said she was willing to help with anything he needed. He thanked her and said he would call soon.

He ate as the coffee brewed and when it was done headed out to the porch to take in the morning. Dr. Hayes had him start doing this each Saturday for the last three months. The good doctor had told him that if he avoided everything that had to do with Ivy then he would not confront his grief. He was right. So every Saturday Paul sat on the front porch and drank a cup of coffee.

As he sat down he heard the sound of laughter from next door. When he turned to look he saw Molly heading toward him. Ben was sitting on the porch watching his daughter while still trying to give her a little space. Ben waved and Paul waved back.

Molly was holding the stuffed dog she seemed to always have with her. She had a smile on her face when she asked, "Is that coffee?" and pointed at his cup.

Paul smiled back. "Yes it is."

Molly nodded a little and said, "Good," and sat down.

Paul looked up at Ben and shrugged. It was the first time Molly had ever sat down next to him. Ivy would color with her sometimes, and they had watched Molly a couple of times when

Marci ran to the store, but it had never been for more than an hour. It was usually Ivy that Molly had interacted with.

She sat next to him and looked out around the neighborhood, absently playing with the ear of her stuffed dog. He took another drink and just watched her for a minute. She seemed relaxed and he wondered if she was waiting for something. After a couple more sips he asked, "What is the dog's name again?" trying to make conversation. Even though Molly appeared completely comfortable just sitting and watching from the porch, Paul wasn't.

"Max," Molly said in reply.

Paul took another couple of sips.

"I have your Jeep in my garage, would you like me to get it?" he asked almost getting up as he spoke.

Molly looked up at him. She had brown hair like her mother's, back in a ponytail and she had little freckles across her nose. Her brown eyes were soft when they met his gaze. "Are you done with your coffee?" she asked back.

He looked in his cup and saw he had a little less than half left. He could have fibbed, but telling a four-year-old something that wasn't true seemed like a bad idea. "Not yet," he said back.

"You should finish your coffee," she said and nodded again. It wasn't an order, but he wondered if all children were that insistent. Paul finally relaxed and finished his cup of coffee.

When he was done he stood up and walked to the garage and opened the door. Paul brought the Jeep out and Molly simply said, "Thank you" and got in and drove back to her house. He waved as she drove away, then grabbed his cup and walked back into the house.

On Monday morning Dr. Hayes asked how things were going. He asked every Monday and Paul usually said simply, "I'm ok, seems a little better." That Monday he told the doctor about Saturday and having his coffee with Molly on the porch. When Paul asked if it was normal for a four year old, the doctor only said, "Children are not always easy to predict. Sometimes they surprise us."

Paul immersed himself again in work for the week. On Saturday as he sat on the porch he saw Molly head over to sit with him again. She brought a juice box this time and seemed to drink it slowly. She didn't say anything. When he was almost done with his coffee Ben strolled up and asked, "Would you like to come to dinner? We are going to do a cookout." Paul said yes and Molly got up and skipped back to her house. Paul watched her go, her father following behind.

She had left her juice box on the porch and he picked it up and walked back into the house, not sure of what to make of what happened.

He needed to get some groceries and drop off dry cleaning so he showered and headed out. It was late in the afternoon when he returned home. He was bringing in bags when his phone rang. It was Marci.

"Hi Paul?" she asked.

"Yes," he said.

"I was just checking to see if you were coming over for some BBQ? It would be nice of you to come by and we have plenty of food." Marci's voice sounded uneven, as if she wasn't sure if she should be asking him.

"Yes, Ben asked this morning. I would be happy to come by," he replied.

"Good then, we will see you at 6," she said and hung up.

He headed over next door right at 6. He had found a bottle of red wine in the cabinet above the fridge and brought it with him.

He was standing on the porch deciding if bowing out might be a better idea when the door swung open. It was Marci.

"Hello Paul," she said.

He smiled. "Hello," he said back. Paul observed Molly walk up behind Marci.

"Ben is out back at the grill," Marci said and gestured for him to come in. He handed her the wine and thanked her again for inviting him.

Molly reached up and put her hand in his and tugged him toward the back door. Paul followed, careful not to squeeze her little hand to hard.

When they walked out back Ben was at the grill and it smelled amazing.

"Hello" Paul said. Ben turned around and extended out his hand. Paul reached out his hand to shake Ben's and let go of Molly's.

Ben smiled. "Marci was very happy to have you come over and join us," he said as he returned to the grill.

"I am happy to be here," Paul said, pretty sure he meant it.

"Would you like a beer?" Ben asked as Molly showed him where he was going to be sitting.

"Sure," Paul said looking around for where he would find the beer.

Ben opened a small cooler near him and pulled out a bottle. Paul took it, removed the cap and took a swig.

"How is everything?" Ben asked. It took Paul a minute to realize that Ben wasn't using the same tone most did with him. Paul had started calling it the 'I'm Sorry' tone which had an insidious way of pulling him into his grief again.

"Things are better," he answered honestly. He went on to tell Ben about the deal he had just closed. Ben told him about a new building he was working on that was being built downtown and was supposed to be as "green" as a building could get.

They talked for about 20 minutes before Marci emerged from the house carrying a salad. She put it down and picked up a platter next to the grill for Ben to put the burgers and what looked like corn and potatoes. Paul watched them interact and felt a small knot form in his stomach. He felt a little hand on his arm.

"Do you like veggies? I think they stink," Molly said.

He looked over at her and it made him smile. He turned back just as Marci brought the items over from the grill.

Paul tried to help but was politely shut down.

They ate and he enjoyed the company. They didn't once ask about Ivy. It was the first dinner out with people he knew, other than for work, where the topic of his wife wasn't brought up once. It was refreshing.

After dinner Molly wandered off to color as Marci and Ben discussed their plans for the house, the weather or the neighbors. They were specifically avoiding topics that would upset him and it made the night enjoyable. It got late and Marci headed in to do dishes and put Molly to bed Paul assumed. He said, "I think I am going to get going, I want to thank you again for inviting me over."

Ben told him, "You are welcome anytime." Since Ben was still putting up some of the items from dinner, Paul said he would show himself out. As he was opening the door, Molly ran up and handed him a paper. "For you," she whispered and looked in the direction of the kitchen before quietly sneaking back upstairs.

He called out "Thanks" to Marci and headed home.

When Paul got into his kitchen he set down the paper on his counter. It was almost an exact copy of the last picture he had been given from Molly. It had a smiling yellow sun and a rainbow and said: Bee Happy.

He snatched his cup and went to grab the bottle sitting on the counter when he paused. He set the cup back down and headed into the living room, picked up the remote, found a movie and settled in for the night.

On Monday, in Dr. Hayes office, Paul told him about his experiences over the weekend. The doctor was pleased to hear that Paul had social interaction outside of co-workers or clients. Paul told the doctor about the call he had received from Barbara and how she had asked about going through Ivy's things.

Dr. Hayes asked him "How do you feel about it?"

Paul thought on it for a minute and replied, "I don't think I am ready."

The doctor seemed to contemplate this for a minute, then asked Paul, "Do you think you will ever be ready to say goodbye?"

Paul was a little stunned by the question and how close it hit home. He hadn't thought about it much, saying goodbye. All he could say was, "I don't think I am ready." It came out in a whisper.

Dr. Hayes tilted his head a little and said, "Her things are not her. Ivy is the memories you have of her and your life together. The stuff is just that, stuff. I am sure there are some sentimental items that you should hold onto, however, you cannot freeze time, Paul."

Paul could tell that the doctor was waiting for his words to sink in. When Paul finally looked up at him, the doctor simply said, "Wait, until you are ready."

Paul called Barbara on Wednesday night. When she answered he told her that she could come over on Saturday for lunch. Barbara thanked him and asked, "Is there was anything I can bring?"

Paul replied, "A few boxes."

Barbara paused for a moment and then said, "I can do that. See you Saturday."

He closed his eyes and felt like he had been holding his breath for the entire phone call. He grabbed his cup, filled it and walked into the living room.

On Saturday morning he walked out to find Molly already sitting on the porch. She had her juice box, Max and a small plastic bag sitting next to her.

As Paul sat down she smiled up at him and yelled, "Happy Saturday!" thrusting her arms in the air.

He smiled and said, "Happy Saturday to you." She smiled back, picked up her juice box and took a sip.

They sat in silence for several minutes watching the street. The sun made the water from an early morning rain glisten off the cars as it filtered through the leaves of the trees that lined the street. Paul turned to look at his small friend.

She turned and met his gaze. "Me, Mom and Daddy are going to the park today, what are you doing?"

"Well," he started, "I have lunch with my mother-in-law today." He tried to not sound sad.

"Sounds fun," was Molly's reply, not seeming to pick up on the feelings welling up inside of him. Paul knew it wouldn't be fun, and he didn't know if he could go through with it. But as Molly sat there looking at him he realized she didn't understand the significance of the lunch or the weight of it. She was four, and it was simple. He was having lunch with his family and it should be fun.

When he finished his coffee and set the cup down Molly stood up and grabbed Max and the bag that had been next to her. She thrust the bag out to Paul. "These are for you." Paul took the bag and opened it. Inside were two oatmeal cookies, which were his favorite. "Mom made them," she said and turned to head back to her house.

"Thank you, Molly," Paul shouted as she ran back to her father who was sitting on their porch reading the paper.

He grabbed up his cup, her empty juice box and headed inside with the cookies to get ready for lunch.

When Barbara pulled into the driveway he felt the knot in his stomach again. He knew he wasn't ready, but Dr. Hayes words had sunk in. It didn't matter if he was ready, it wasn't about him. It was about Ivy.

Barbara greeted him with a hug. Paul had picked up supplies for sandwiches for lunch. He didn't have an appetite and it turned out that neither did Barbara.

He helped her grab the boxes she had left in her car. She told him she wasn't sure if he was really ready. "I didn't want to upset you," she had said with tears on the edges of her eyes. He had to remember he wasn't the only one who had lost someone. He hugged her again and began to build the boxes and tape the bottoms.

Barbara noticed the picture of the sun on his counter and held it up. "It is from Molly, next door," he told her. She smiled and put it on the fridge under a magnet from the local pizza delivery place.

"Where do you want to start?" Barbara asked.

"The closet," he said and grabbed a couple of boxes. For the next few hours Paul found himself on an internal roller coaster of emotions. Every item had a memory.

Barbara made sure that he knew that if there was anything he wanted to keep he should just set it aside. He wanted to keep everything; instead he kept a t-shirt from Ivy's college that she wore to bed during the winter. When he held it to his face he could smell her. He walked into the other room and felt the tears. Barbara came and sat with him putting her arms around him. "That is enough for today," she said pulling him close.

"Thank you," he said nodding.

He helped her get the filled boxes to the car. When he

went back inside he saw the bag from Molly on the kitchen counter. He grabbed it and headed into his bedroom. He sat on the bed holding the shirt and eating the cookies. Ivy used to make cookies for him as a surprise. He smiled when he remembered when he asked her why she didn't make them all the time. Her reply was, "Because if you had them all the time they wouldn't be a treat. A treat is a special thing for sometimes."

Ivy had been a treat.

On Sunday he worked on going through Ivy's things by himself. He went through her drawers and packed up her colorful sock collection. He packed away her yearbooks and mementos of her friends from school. He knew Barbara would know who to share those with. He found a shoe box in the top part of the closet. When he opened it he found it was full of cards. They were all cards he had given her. She had saved them. He closed the box and put it back on the shelf. He was done for the day.

Dr. Hayes was very pleased with what Paul had accomplished. Paul was a little proud that he was able to share what he had done when it had seemed so far off just one week before. Dr. Hayes asked him what his next step was. Paul replied, "Keep going I guess." Dr. Hayes nodded.

The weeks got better. Molly was there each Saturday morning and he found himself looking forward to the simplicity of sitting with her. It had been a month since Barbara's visit and Paul asked her to return to help him complete packing everything up.

At the end of the day they had managed to pack up everything with the exception of the box of cards that was sitting on the top of the shelf in the bedroom. It was the last piece but the one that he believed would be the most difficult for him. He elected to wait just one more week.

During the next session Dr. Hayes asked him if he wanted to space out his sessions further. The doctor felt that Paul was in a better place, and that he wasn't crippled by his grief anymore. Paul agreed, he could spread out the appointments to once a month and if any issues arose he would call.

The week seemed to sail by and on Saturday morning he

woke up to rain. He opened the front door with the thought that he might see Molly sitting and waiting. She wasn't there. He was a little disappointed. He had gotten a couple of cupcakes for them to share. Since Molly had brought cookies once, it only seemed fair.

He pulled the box down from the shelf and brought it to the kitchen, poured himself another cup of coffee and opened it.

The box contained every card or note he had ever sent Ivy. He had no idea she had saved them. The first one on top was from Valentine's Day. It had candy hearts, one of which had a bite out of it. On the inside it said "Sweet as Candy" and he had signed it, "Love You Always – PBJ". He set down the card on the counter. He picked up and read every card, one after the other, traveling through some of the very best moments of their life together.

He had begun to cry, but after while it became easier. He started to remember her smile. He was most of the way through the box when he was reading a funny "Thinking of You" card when it hit him that Ivy, his Ivy, would be upset thinking he was in this state because of her. She would want him to celebrate her, to celebrate *them*. He smiled then, closing his eyes and imagining her chastising him.

He picked up the last card in the box. It had a bee on the cover and when he opened it, the entire inside of the card was a smiling sun with a rainbow behind it. It said "Bee Happy" in large letters and was signed, "I want to always make you smile – PBJ". Paul looked up from the card to the fridge where Molly's picture was.

He got the picture off the fridge and held it side by side next to the card. He put them on the counter and put all the other cards back into the box.

It had stopped raining. He looked back at the card and the picture on the counter, grabbed the cupcakes off the counter and headed out the door.

He knocked on the door a couple of times before Marci answered.

"Is Molly here?" Paul asked. "I brought her some cupcakes," he said and held them out.

Marci looked at him in confusion as she reached and took the package from Paul's outstretched hand. Shaking her head slightly she said, "I'm sorry, she isn't home. I will give them to her when she gets back. I am sure she will love them."

"When will she be home?" Paul blurted out, more aggressively than he'd intended.

Marci took a half step back and said, "Paul, Molly is at her grandparent's house. She is there every Saturday."

"Every Saturday?" he asked.

"Yes, we take her there first thing in the morning and pick her up Sunday afternoon. Are you ok, Paul?" Marci asked.

"I'm fine," he said as he backed off the porch.

As he stumbled back to his house he began to replay the last time he had seen Molly. She had been there on the porch, with Max. He shook his head as if the memory would fade.

He pulled out his cell phone and frantically dialed Dr. Hayes. As it rang, he wondered what he should say. What *could* he say?

His heart began to beat faster and he stopped, resting his hands on his knees trying to slow his breathing. His throat tightened. He couldn't understand what was happening. Was he crazy? Had he imagined everything? He closed his eyes. This can't be happening, he thought. He heard the voicemail for Dr. Hayes office through the phone in his hand and pushed the end call button.

He needed to sit down. He just needed rest, he thought. He knew it had been an emotional day and had taken a lot out of him. He would call Dr. Hayes in the morning and set up an appointment, explain in person. He would have time to figure it all out by then. It would be ok.

As he approached his porch he saw the little pink car parked right at the bottom step. He looked up to see Molly sitting and eating a cupcake. When she saw him she smiled, frosting all around her mouth. He smiled back and knew everything would be ok.

<<<◇>>>

About Erika Lance

I would say I was fortunate, some would say otherwise, to have a chance to live across the US. Originally from Minneapolis, MN I spent most of my formative years in Hollywood, CA, then NM, CO, GA, WI and FL. Moving around a lot meant I got to see so many interesting parts of our country and the cultures that are all around us. All through my life I was lucky to have many artists; writers, actors, painters, poets and musicians. It made for a very wild upbringing. I grew up as an elusive female nerd. My head was either buried in a book or playing RPGs (if your cool you know what that means), it made for an imaginative existence. My love of writing started at a young age and although I wrote a lot for myself, it took hitting that certain moment in my life to decide I wanted to share my universe with the world. With that said, it will most likely be an amazing ride so old on tight.

Connect with Erika:
www.erikalance.com
Email: erikalance@gmail.com
Facebook.com/Erika-Lance
Twitter.com/AuthorELance
Instagram.com/AuthorELance

Other books by Erika Lance
On the Verge (Anthology)
Behind the Veil (Anthology)
The Death of Jimmy (Anthology)
Into the Abyss (Anthology)

Ruby Dust

By Lisa Barry

Ghirn shuffled aimlessly along the dirt road, leaving a trail of red dust behind him, much to chagrin of the lovely ladies loitering in front of The Pink House where no shenanigans happen, ever. He snorted quietly to himself and forced his thoughts to his wife and daughter who were vacationing on Kandra Three with Soli's parents. Ghirn wasn't sad to be left behind on Mars. Soli's dad was a real jerk to put it mildly, and took the protective streak of a gargoyle to a whole new level. No, it was Niema his daughter that he missed. Her cute little wings, thick, chubby cheeks and her horns only just starting to come in; she was already a ferocious little guard.

Hoping for some peace that evening, maybe a raw tundle bird and some hot vinegar, Ghirn continued his shuffle down the street, tail whipping behind him. His stomach grumbled and he realized quitting time wasn't far off. He'd missed lunch earlier due to the Bandlaud twins getting into Hep's tundle bird trap again. They were more work than Bucca, who kept robbing the local treasury. He *always* got caught. Ghirn could out fly the moron's bull any day.

A pounding in the distance made Ghirn pause his thoughts. He turned to see a small dust cloud making its way toward the only nearby mountain. There were rumors that the summit had a safe place for outlaws, but Ghirn was pretty sure it was bull dross.

Watching the dust cloud, Ghirn sighed. It looked like the day would be longer than he thought. He quickened his pace a skotch, only stopping once to holler at Hep, the butcher, to save him a bird. Someone who had visited Earth had thought it would be funny to create the city after the ancient Wild West stories, the geography being mildly similar. He wondered who the joke was on when the damn town exploded with less than admirable dealings and business whatnots.

Decision made, Ghirn jumped into the air again. He flew leisurely toward the travelling dust. He did some flips and some infinity eights. He flew up a few hundred feet and then free fell for a while, catching himself at the last moment and banked left, where he scooped Bucca and his bag of loot off his bull.

Bucca didn't even bother fighting, an old game that neither of them was excited about any more. He just folded his scaled arms over his chest and hung upside-down in one of Ghirn's foot claws, his breathing tube hanging below his head. Ghirn couldn't see Bucca's eyes due to the fancy copper goggles the kid wore over his thick rubbery face. His mouth was just a seam closed tight around his breather. Poor kid had to wear it all the time since neither Mars air nor Earth air were a good fit. Ghirn was hard pressed to remember what planet Bucca was from.

Ghirn held the bag of various denominations used throughout the universes. It was a good size take. Ghirn blew a stream from his nose as he shook his head and headed toward the jail. Bucca worked at the only mechanic shop in town and he was a surprisingly good engineer but for some reason he kept hitting up the Treasury. Ghirn wondered if visits to the saloon were the culprit. The wind was loud as they soured hundreds of feet above dusty ground, and his ears popped when he reentered the town's air pocket. He released his lungs from stone and took in a full breath.

As if it were practiced, Bucca held out a hand as they headed down to the rooftop of the jail. Ghirn grasped it and let go of Bucca's foot. He stretched his claw a bit to work out the beginnings of a cramp just before landing with a thump on the roof. He let go of Bucca's hand and pulled open the hatch that opened above the jail room.

Glimpsing the soft mattress and quiet quarters inside, Ghirn stood up and met the youngster's eyes. Bucca lifted the breather from his mouth and smiled. Ghirn saw the sharp yellow teeth that hid beneath his pleasant exterior. Then it hit him. He laughed and laughed, doubling over before finally catching his breath and patting Bucca on the shoulder. Bucca's smile was wide now.

"It took me a while," he said to Bucca as he took the kids hand and lowered him into the jail room. Bucca waved but never said a word as Ghirn closed the hatch. He thought of poor old Scholuta who ran the Treasury and wondered if he had any idea that Bucca's shenanigans were purely for the promise of a sky ride with a gargoyle.

Ghirn tilted his head and looked past the brim of his hat in an old fashion attempt to read the time using the sun. Though the sun was sagging low in the horizon, it wasn't what he ended up looking at. His shoulders slumped as he watched fire bursts and small explosions caused by someone coming into the atmosphere, too fast and without a clue.

He jumped over the side of the building, landed with a poof of red dust and walked into the Sheriff's office. He went right up to the front desk, skirted around and kicked the leg of the chair where Snicks sat, head hung back, drool glistening just under his extraordinarily large orange nose. Snicks' head rolled up like a cart wheel over a bump. The thick drool, now pushed heavily into the old rogues windpipe, had him coughing and sputtering his nasty spit all over the damn place.

While he waited for Snicks, a rotund creature from one of the Sierrnean populated star clusters, to get a grip, Ghirn glanced at the viewer. Once again Snicks had been eavesdropping on the Earth people's strange infatuation with reality shows. He didn't recognize the family having a food fight on the large screen.

"What the hell, Ghi!" Snicks growled, finally coherent.

"Stop sleeping and watching TV on my time."

"Well, what the hell else am I supposed to do around here? Since you done came here ain't nobody hardly doing anything. It's boring as hell."

Sighing, Ghirn patted the man gently on the back while he also deposited the bag of loot he'd taken from Bucca onto the desk. A curl of smoke left his nose and Snicks leaned away. Snicks had been on Mars for ages and was hardened against most things, but apparently he hadn't forgotten what Ghirn could do when he was pissed. That time. Once. A few months back.

"Try calling Hank and getting him in the direction of that way," Ghirn said and pointed south. "We got a hot one coming in."

"Well whoopty doo," Snicks said and reached over to press a button on his comm. Ghirn pressed a different button on the main system console and the viewer switched from Earth reality TV to the security cameras. He quickly minimized the town views, all twenty-four of them and switched to the satellite.

It was pointing the wrong way. Muttering soft threats, he set it to re-align and glanced at the sleepmonger who hadn't been checking on them. Snicks was chatting amicably on the comm about which carriage Hank should take to the crash site. Ghirn snorted a bit of steam. Snicks quickly ended off and put a buzz into Accidents.

The satellite aligned and Ghirn was finally able to see the accident waiting to happen. He frowned and leaned in closer to the screen.

"You can expand it," Snicks said while motioning in the air. The image grew, making Ghirn step back.

"I *know* that, Snicks." His eyes never left the screen. "Dang. Is that what I think it is?"

Snicks looked, his brows furrowing in doubt. "But we haven't seen nothing like that since I was a newb."

"For being the softest and easiest to kill species I know of, humans sure can get themselves into more difficulties..."

"You sure that's human?"

"As sure as that knob on your face keeps you breathing."

"Well," Snicks whispered. "You'd better get on over there. The Dearndins sure like themselves a tasty human."

Ghirn moaned. He'd forgotten that little tidbit, and they had three of them on planet at the moment. Nice, quiet, human-eating little Dearndins.

"On my way now," he said heading to the door.

"Accidents will be out to ya shortly," Snicks hollered behind him.

As soon as he was outside, Ghirn tightened the string to keep his hat on tight and pushed his leathery wings out. They didn't have bats on Mars but he knew that's what the humans would liken his wings to. He also knew that sending a gargoyle to greet a human was going to be interesting to say the least.

He hopped into the air and with a few hard flaps was speeding over the crusty ruby colored ground. He heard the faintest pop when he passed through the shield that camouflaged the town from prying eyes and circulated the oxygen rich air. The air of Mars itself wasn't breathable unless you were lucky enough to turn your lungs to stone. Ghirn hardened his lungs and windpipe as he flew. The human wouldn't last but a couple of minutes without oxygen. He hoped Accidents didn't forget to bring some along.

The small spacecraft was spinning through the sky now. Ghirn sped up to help break some of the impact. When he reached it and grabbed a wing of the heavy vessel, he let it pull him along for a few turns before reversing the pull, using his wings as a virtual lever. Slowly the craft came out of its spin and Ghirn was able to take a little bit of the edge off the crash.

After it settled, leaving a thick veil of dust in the air, he could hear the insides creak and tumble about like a tundle bird in a box. Ghirn blinked his eyes and remembered once more that he was quite hungry. A flash of a memorable dinner at his Gramp's house on Earth made his stomach clench.

He watched Hank's team from a distance. It looked like they brought one of the newer steambed carriages this time. He nodded his approval to no one in particular and squinted in the distance looking for Accidents. In his haste, he had forgotten to ask if they were flying or land cruising. Either way, they shouldn't be too much behind Hank.

The humans, though he didn't actually know how many were in there, hadn't opened up the door yet but he could hear movement long after the dust had settled. He wondered if he should leave and let the boys take care of it. He had done his part after all.

A flash of motion appeared in the cockpit window. Ghirn faintly heard a holler and something crashed inside. He decided to back up. A lot. The crack in their hull was going to bring them out soon enough. Hitting the sky with a flap of his wings, he waved at Hank as he flew by and then waved again at Accidents just as their land cruiser caught up and surpassed Hank. He landed at a point where the human would just see a blob in the distance even though he could see just fine.

Accidents was a group of three...

Ghirn struggled to give them a name. They were just blobby weird creatures. They didn't speak but communicated using pictures. It was a strange but workable system.

They could help anyone because they sent out pictures of what they needed or wanted. So assuming the creature, or person, wasn't completely bull dross scared out of their minds, they could get the help they needed. Accidents looked like the red jello Earthlings seemed to enjoy so much and Hank, well Hank resembled what they called a gronilla. Or was it gorilda? It had been some time since he'd visited Gramps.

He knew it wouldn't be long now. He guessed they had about ten minutes before the air in that craft wasn't going to support them. He sat in the hot sand and watched the sun touch the horizon. It was about to get unbearably sticky and hot out here. He could see the mechanical arm of Hank's steam-bed rising up slowly. No one liked to get stuck outside at night. The heat was miserable. Frowning, Ghirn thought about Accidents. He wondered if they got less solid in the heat.

A single astronaut came out of the craft wearing the typical human body gear. He held a large firearm and walked ever so slowly backward. Accidents got to work. Ghirn imagined them showing the person how nice it was inside their vehicle, or perhaps the large smiling gargoyle that wanted to help them. He chortled but forgot that his lungs were stone. It didn't have quite the same affect. He shrugged and kept watching.

The human lowered his gun and seemed to be taking stock of the situation. Accidents was probably showing him, or her Ghirn supposed, images of dying without oxygen and taking the tank and hose that they were offering. With their globular arms. And no eyes. Ghirn wondered which one of them was really scarier to the human; him or them. Maybe the images they sent out made the human think they looked differently. Now wouldn't that be something.

Probably in desperation, the human finally lowered his

weapon and accepted the breather and tank. After taking a long pull of air, it pointed to the breather and then toward the craft and then pointed back at itself.

One of Accidents crew looked through the door and turned abruptly. Ghirn knew damn well it had no eyes but he'd be darned if it didn't look straight at him. An image of a body trapped under equipment popped into his head. Why the heck Hank couldn't handle that he had no idea except that it was getting dark and Hank *was* working on removing the ugly craft from the sand.

Ghirn jumped into the air and possibly gave the little human a heart attack when he landed at the door of the crash and peered inside. Sure enough, there was another human, pinned down by part of an inside wall. He couldn't really fit through the doorway so he reached in and lifted the wall with one hand, then contorted slightly to grab an arm and pulled the body out.

Accidents moved in like crocskunks, shoving open the helmet and sticking the breather in the human's mouth. When nothing happened, Ghirn slapped the human's chest, gently of course, which caused it take in a long breath. Ghirn smiled and nodded his head. *I'm good for some things* he thought.

Then the human saw him, spat out the breather while screaming and tried to scoot away with an obvious broken leg. Ghirn sunk down glumly onto his haunches.

The other human got it to calm down until finally everyone was mostly happy again. Ghirn helped Hank load up the craft and as the sun disappeared, Accidents got the humans into the land cruiser.

Despite the intense heat that fell over the planet during the night, Ghirn enjoyed his easy flight back, looking forward to finally getting dinner and maybe getting to read a few pages of the new book his wife had sent over from Kandra Three.

He landed just outside the city and waited for Accidents. When they arrived, the human with the broken leg had already been fixed up and they both had removed their helmets. Males, both of them. Good size as far as Ghirn could judge. They raised their brows at Accidents and Ghirn was betting that they got the picture that they could remove the breathers now. One of them, the one who had come out of the aircraft first, removed his breather and took a tentative breath.

With a smile to the other, the human handed his breather and tank back to Accidents. A picture popped into Ghirn's head of the humans eating. He whipped a look at Accidents and the same picture popped in again except with even more food in it. Ghirn fought the urge to sag and melt into the ground. Not that he could, but it would have been nice.

But of course, who else would ensure the humans had food and rest while Hank fixed up their craft so they could get them the heck out of here.

The first human walked right up to Ghirn and held out his hand. Ghirn chuckled and a curl of smoke left his nose. The human didn't budge and Ghirn was impressed. He took the man's hand and gave it a shake. He thought the human might have looked a bit surprised that he knew the gesture but hey, he shrugged, these things get around. He watched Accidents drive off, probably laughing at him.

Ghirn reached up and flicked the switch on the bronze translator hooked to his collar.

"Welcome to Ruby Dust," he said.

"You speak English?" the first man said, stunned. Literally. Like he wouldn't keep walking.

"Yes, yes. Now come on. We have a meal to get to. We have many things you will probably like."

The man closed his mouth and started walking. The other man glanced around warily. Ghirn wondered if he was like the scientist guy while the other was the happy, pilot face of the camera guy.

"This looks like an old wild west town, Mike." The second human spoke for the first time, at least in Ghirn's hearing.

"I know, it's bizarre," Mike said.

"It was designed after one of your old towns," Ghirn said.

The second man shook his head as if he was trying to clear away a bad memory. Ghirn was hesitant to point out The Pink House, though the loitering, half-dressed ladies probably gave them a clue.

He heard the noise just before a body came flying out of the saloon and slammed to the dirt in front of him. Ghirn cocked his head and blew a stream of smoky dust from his nose as he looked at the alien before him. Dark purple skin, four legs, big yellow eyes. One of which was blinking profusely. It's oddly shaped chops had a white fluid dripping from it. Ghirn wasn't sure if it was blood or spit. He was surprised the Dearndin was even in the saloon as the species usually kept to itself.

"How dare they treat me with such disrespect?! Sheriff, I implore you to arrest the entire staff." The Dearndin folded its arms over its chest and Ghirn noted that it, he, had six fingers on each hand. He glanced at the feet and confirmed six toes on each. Ghirn wondered how their evolution had come about as he turned to meet eyes with the proprietor of Intergalactic Sauce Tanks Saloon, IST for short.

"Lidry?"

The soft, sing songy voice of the Charfnet started up. He looked human except for the faint blue tinge to his skin. That and the fact that his head was smaller and disproportionate compared to the rest of the body. He was the only Charfnet that Ghirn knew so he wasn't sure if that was standard issue or not.

Lidry could lull you to sleep with his pretty sounds and then take you for everything you were worth. You'd bloody well feel good about it when you woke to boot. As much as Ghirn would have liked to pummel the guy into a pulp of sky blue soup, no one had ever complained. At least, not until now.

Lidry's body moved ever so carefully, in planned and concise, amicable gestures. Ghirn waited for something useful to actually come out the Charfnet's mouth. When nothing did, he resorted to interruption.

"Shut up, Lidry. You're spouting a bunch a bull dross. I'm immune to your stupid charms, so just tell me. Did you refuse the kid service or what?"

"I most certainly did. Everyone knows that the Dearndin do not partake in the tank."

"Everyone knows, huh?" Ghirn sure as hells didn't know, but that would explain why they kept to themselves generally. He often wondered why the Dearndin's ever even stopped in to

Mars. This was a place to toughen up, to grow a pair, or more depending. Ghirn didn't want to think about why he had ended up there with his family.

"I do what I want!" the Dearndin hollered. He pulled out a Cortali 360 ray gun. One of the humans behind Gurin squealed. Ghirn couldn't remember human male's squealing like babies from his short visits to Earth as he stoned his body up enough to protect himself, and reached for the gun. He didn't get there before the first shot was loose.

Lidry was fast enough though, and the laser only put a hole in the pretty sign over the IST.

"Why you...!" Lidry growled.

Ghirn plucked the gun from the Dearndin's hand just as Lidry threw himself at the shooter, fists flying.

"Lidry," Ghirn stated and narrowed his eyes. The man stood and lifted his arms in defeat. Ghirn wondered how much, if any, of the Charfnet was human. He had kind of missed humans. They were an odd lot but quite endearing. He raised his brows and turned to look at the two humans.

They weren't there.

He abruptly remembered that little tidbit about the Dearndin's eating habits and glanced back at the one who'd been thrown out of the IST. The creature gave him a facial waggle that Ghirn took to be bad omen. It was the scream from inside The Pink House that led him in the right direction.

The ladies scattered when he came through the front door, accidently knocking off part of the door trim. One Dearndin held the first human, Mike, against the back wall. He had clearly bitten the man's neck and was licking the blood while holding a hand over the man's mouth. The man's eyes were wild with fear but he was alive so that was a good thing. The second Dearndin had the other human on the floor and was sniffing his hand.

Steam poured from Ghirn's mouth. The heat in his stomach, fed by his missed dinner and the fact that these idiot's had pulled a fast one on him, burned up his throat.

"Not the furniture, Ghi!" one of the ladies screeched at him. He thought her name was Filly. He took in a deep breath and let the heat settle back down. Wouldn't help him get off this planet if he blew up again.

Instead, he scooped up a leg of one Dearndin and the arm of the other and dragged them out of the house. He then dragged them all the way to the office. Snitch was snogging one of the girls from The Pink House. She jumped up, curtsied to Ghirn and ran out the door. Snitch let Bucca go and helped him lock up the Dearndin's.

"I want the other one found and put in with the rest of them. Then I want a posting that eating other visitors is strictly forbidden. I want their..." Ghirn pointed an angry thumb at the jail, "departure to be recorded when I send them off planet and it should be part of the post. Got it?"

"Yessir," Snitch said with a heavy nod.

When Ghirn got back to The Pink House, the ladies were crooning. The two humans looked stricken as they sat solidly on a stiff backed couch. Far from titillating, the ladies were trying to offer teas and snacks but they had no idea what humans might like to eat. He only had to see the motion in one of the bowls and scent the muddy flavor of the shiarta plant from Pluto to know they had it very wrong.

Snorting the last vestiges of anger through his nose, he motioned for the humans to come. They spared no time in jumping up and following. If he wasn't so hungry, Ghirn just might have been amused. He led the human's behind the IST and went into the back room. This time, he managed to leave the door trim intact.

He was pleased to see that Lidry had come through. Ghirn knew that watching him eat a live tundle bird would likely seriously harm the mental situation of his guests so instead, a full bird had been super cooked and dressed and now closely resembled a chicken, just like they had on Earth. One of the humans, the one not called Mike, let out a sigh and stepped to the table.

Ghirn waved for them to be seated as he settled himself at the table across from them. Not bothering with a chair, he just went to stone from the waist down.

Something resembling salad was on the table, as well as some trukka beans and horned squash. The humans, apparently starting to go immune to the different world around them, dug in. A silent buzz filled the air while they ate, installing the life force that only sustenance can provide. Ghirn shoveled the bird meat, only mildly missing the dribble of fresh blood down his chin and he suddenly missed his little Niema. She would have been thrilled to meet real live humans. Especially after the stories that he told her that Gramps had told him.

He was contemplating licking his plate, the humans were still slowly chewing their beans with expressions that Ghirn didn't understand, when a soft knock pulled his attention away. He unlocked his stone legs and went to the door, narrowly escaping a bump on the head from the low ceilings.

Hank stood there with a goofy smile. His wide mouth and block shaped teeth were so different to Ghirn's pointed mouth and sharp teeth. *Something to do with their diet preferences?* Ghirn wondered. He realized he didn't know *what* Hank ate. He would have to have him over for dinner one day.

"Their vessel is fixed," Hank said. He had a bit of a lisp Ghirn noticed for the first time. "I've already alerted Accidents."

Ghirn nodded. Good, that made his life easier. He thanked Hank and sunk back down at the table, waiting for the humans to finish.

"Was that an ape?" Mike asked.

"I think it was a gorilla," the other said.

"Seriously, Joe? What's the difference?" Mike had a hint of a smile. Amazing what food will do for a person.

"If you boys are ready, your craft has been repaired."

The human called Joe cocked his head. Mike asked, "Ready? How is that possible?"

Ghirn shrugged and when the humans shrank back, he realized his gesture might not communicate what he meant.

"Hank is very talented and has the latest equipment. He would probably even upgrade it if he were allowed."

"That is amazing," Mike said, his eyes like saucers. Joe looked a little doubtful, but Ghirn only cared about getting them to their ship and on their way. He was ready for this day to be over. One of the bar maids took that moment to saunter in. A cute girl from the Vergio Lux galaxy, she had the unmistakable translucent skin and large orange reptilian eyes. Vergio's made great bar aids because they had four arms. Extremely capable in the service industry. She managed to get all the plates and serving dishes onto two trays while the humans gawked, and then left the room.

"She's a pretty one, isn't she?" Ghirn mused out loud. The humans brought their wide eyes to Ghirn. Did they agree or not agree? Ghirn couldn't tell. He finally got them out of the IST and was pleased to see that Accidents was there with the land cruiser.

After some hand shaking, he turned the humans over. He would watch take off before he would leave. He wasn't sure if the other Dearndin had been found and he didn't want to lose the humans now.

Ghirn jumped into the air and as soon as he left the protection of the shield, the heat smashed into him. He was able to control his skin, and thereby his temperature, but that didn't mean it was comfortable. Thank goodness the shield had been put in place.

At the launch pad, the humans were escorted into their ship by a couple of Grembles, Sudinacow and Sharlimut. They were twin brothers who had night shift at the launch pad. They were from some planet that was hotter than blazes and the Mars atmosphere didn't seem to affect them, so the job worked out for them. Ghirn couldn't help but wonder if they would ever leave and have a family or if they were drifters. He was too nice to ask such prying questions. Maybe he would have to have them over for lunch one day, too. It was high time he got to know his peers better.

He hung out near the main office and watched as the ship lifted off and made its way through the atmosphere. He waited just a bit longer to make sure they didn't come back. Accidents had done their mind magic and set it up so that after the humans got back into space, all they would remember was visiting the planet, finding it uninhabitable, collecting some soil and rocks and going home. It was safest for everybody if they just forgot the details. Humans weren't quite ready for the universe, Ghirn guessed.

When his comm went off, Ghirn was sunken down in the living area of his home, the big screen in front of him, trying to decide if he wanted hot vinegar or not. He clicked his comm.

"Caller from Kandra Three," the comm announced. Ghirn smiled. "Accepted."

His lovely wife appeared on the screen, her tuft of white hair decorated with gems. His heart lurched.

"Ghirn, I miss you," she said. Her hand touched the screen in front of her.

"I miss you too, love. I don't know if I can wait another month."

She laughed. A smaller head poked up from the right of the screen.

"Hi, Daddy!" Niema said. She was obviously trying to see into the screen better. Ghirn gazed at her, smiling.

"Are you day dreaming again?" she asked. Ghirn chuckled.

"You know, my girls. Just another day in Ruby Dust."

About Lisa Barry

Growing up in Florida was not a good enough reason for author, Lisa Barry, to avoid wearing black. A daily color choice, Lisa constantly pines for cool enough weather to wear boots.

Living with her supportive (and hot) husband and amazingly awesome kidlets, Lisa counts it a blessing that they still love her despite the deafening sound of her music muse throughout the house.

Writing and reading every minute she can, Lisa counts on the cats to keep her keyboard warm and on the countless gargoyles who listen carefully when she reads to them aloud.

Connect with Lisa online:
www.lisa-barry.com
Email: authorlisabarry@gmail.com
twitter.com/authorlisabarry
facebook.com/authorlisabarry

Other books by Lisa Barry
Rogue (Book Two of the Gargoyles Den Series)
The Guardians (Book One of the Gargoyles Den Series)
On the Verge (Anthology)
Behind the Veil (Anthology)
The Death of Jimmy (Anthology)
Into the Abyss (Anthology)
Beyond the Threshold (Anthology)

My Last Run

By Rhiannon Matlock

Minutes. That's all that I had left. My little sister had taken the abuse for me but that was going to end here. Now.

I adjusted a few settings on the dials of the ancient pod before I looked out at the horizon that was my destiny. Before me were millions of stars, and I was hurtling through space so quickly that any variation could fling the pod off course and send it crashing into oblivion. Just like me I thought.

Though I couldn't see them, six other cruisers flanked me, three on either side. I'd gotten front and center on account of my record being what it was. Also, Mick Forgen, the man who'd organized the competition, had been paid off big time. That wasn't my current concern however. I had maybe a few thousand yards before I would either splat or just skim the surface of that patch of death below.

I'd read about Hell in the old books. Some distant, undefined place where the Devil resided. No matter how bad it was, Hell had nothing on the hot, dark blaze that I was headed for. Burning at over 3000 degrees and so fiery, it turned everything and anything that touched it to ash, even the atmosphere around it. As a result, space around the fiery ball of dead planet was as black as sin and as wide as the eye could see.

Pilots called it the Last Land because it was the last thing that the first explorers saw, and it was the only patch of stars that no one ever went to unless they wanted to kill themselves. Or if they wanted to win a bet.

Racing headlong at oblivion and then turning at the last second was a great way to make a lot of money in a hurry. If you had the guts for it, of course. Rich people with nothing better to do paid a lot of money to see some idiot turn themselves into cinder. Bets large enough to buy luscious planets were placed on who would live or die.

It was a titillating rush, like nothing in the universe. It left your body humming for weeks and feeling like you conquered the world. I'd done this run before. Many times, though I hadn't done it in several years and was a little rusty as a result. I'd let the idiots on my sides catch up to me several times after we'd punched the gas off the starting line. But flying was like breathing to me. Despite the fact I was in a tired, decrepit machine that had bits falling off of it as I pushed it beyond it's limits, I'd caught and overtaken the quicker birds out there.

If you wanted the prize money, you had to survive the gravity force of the planet and be the first one to do it. There was usually only one survivor in this race, but in the event there were more, you wanted to reach the Limit before anyone else. I was seconds from hitting it.

There was a beeping sound. Something else had just malfunctioned on me. I cursed but kept the pressure up. The Limit was the outer ring of the dead planet and, like a vacuum, you had to punch past the force of it. Once you did, it would sling shot your hot little ass with such fierce speed toward the ball of fire that you had mere seconds to pull up, giving you the last run.

Many turned back before they reached the Limit. Once you crossed it, there was no turning back; you were either dust or you made it. Playing chicken with a fiery ball of death. My kind of game.

The outer ring of the Limit was coming up fast, rattling my little ship as it tried to shove me back. I grabbed the stick between my legs and kept her as steady as possible. With a final jolt that lifted me out of my seat and smacked me against the roof of the tiny pod, I slugged through, breaking the last barrier.

Breathing easier, I let off the stick and shoved up my speed. There was no steering at this point, just waiting while you charged through the force and clanged around like a baby's toy.

I readjusted myself and sat back. This was the worse part. Everything slowed and for a few precious moments, I was left with only myself.

The problem was too much time allowed for too much reflection. This was my final run. No matter what happened, it was over after this. Could I live with the consequences if I turned around? The mere fact that I had the thought crushed me. My moment of truth was here and I had doubts. I wanted to cry at the knowledge. Why? Why was I born such a coward?

Liquid eased from my hairline and slid down my face, burning a trail as if to remind me of my sins. I wasn't religious but I knew there were forces beyond me that had set this up. No one gets away with hiding for as long as I had and not pay for it.

With nothing to do, I re-gripped the control stick between my legs, tightened my fingers inside my gloves and waited to break through the other side of the Limit. Why couldn't someone just have killed me already? I thought as I looked at the piece of rock in front of me that had no possibility of survival, even on a good day.

A loud, clanging ring rattled throughout the tin can I was in. A call was coming through. Of all the fucking things to still be working. I didn't want to talk to whoever the hell it was. Let it ring till I burned up in the ash below.

The gods had another plan.

"Hello?" came a shaky, female voice.

The voice was muffled as it spat out from the ancient voice box but I'd know it anywhere. It was my sister. My breath caught in my dry throat and settled harshly against my lungs. I smashed my hand against the controllers, sparking a few circuits that I probably needed, but I didn't care. She was the absolute last sound I wanted to hear right then.

"Brother?" she called out again, a little more desperate this time. "Are you there?"

Silence followed as she waited for me to reply. I couldn't though. Talking to her would only hurt her.

"Dammit Bastian, answer me. I know you're there. I can hear you breathing."

It was a lie. Of sorts. She couldn't technically hear me over so shitty a connection, but we were twins and we'd always had a special bond.

"Bastian," she pleaded and I could hear the grief in her voice. "Talk to me."

Tears came to my eyes and I couldn't fight it. The anxiety and torment I felt wasn't just mine any more. She must've sensed my deteriorating resolve to ignore her because she added one of her patented "please's" that I could never deny. Wiping the water that had somehow made its way into my eyes, I finally answered her.

"Hey," I said, my voice thick even to my own ears.

"Hey," she replied and her relief was palpable to me. "Where are you?"

I didn't answer and my silence must've been enough. I could feel her anger and it was enormous.

"You fucking idiot, what the hell are you doing?" she yelled and her voice reverberated off of everything in the cockpit, including the inside of my skull.

"I had to," I croaked out.

"No, no you didn't," she replied firmly. "You turn your ass right around and you get back here."

I snorted. "You know, for a younger sister you are really bossy."

My attempt at levity was not well met.

"I swear to the Gods Sebastian Reynolds, I will hunt you into every life you have after this if you don't return to me right this minute."

I looked out at the sea of stars. I had no plans to follow her order but I needed an excuse and I found one.

"I can't," I stated simply.

"Yes, you can. I know you can."

"Dials are going wild sis, I have no more control."

"You could fly a horse underwater if you needed to brother, so don't give me that bullshit," she said.

She was right, of course. It had always been thus with us but I couldn't let her win this time. Just a few more seconds.

"Bastian," she warned, but it was too late, I'd just punched through the other end of the Limit.

It was now or never. I licked my lips. I had to make a decision and quick, but all I could see was the blood covering her body and the ultimatum I'd been given. Race one final time and instead of pulling out at the last second like everyone who was watching was betting on, I was to go down in a blaze of glory. Only it was no kind of glory that I'd ever wanted for myself. My consolation was that it would finally free my sister. My craft jerked violently and then started to bang around wildly. A sudden sense of clarity and certainty hit me. There had never really been any hesitation in my mind. I was going to do this. A weight that I couldn't hardly believe lifted from my chest and I smiled.

"I'm not turning back, Belly," I said quietly and set the final course.

I sighed as I let go of the stick and sat back in the shitty seat, letting my head fall against the cracked and beaten head rest. I was charging at a mad rate toward the Last Land.

The ground was coming up far too quickly and I knew that I should be panicking, but instead all I felt was an odd sort of peace. It was here. My end was finally here. I could finally leave it all behind and I didn't have to keep fighting it. I'd cause no more pain.

"You never caused me pain brother," she said suddenly, hearing my thoughts as clearly as if they were her own.

Her voice was thick again, anger leaving her and a new wave of desperation rolled over me. I knew it was hers but it didn't deter me. I was going to save her.

"No Bas," she said harshly and I knew she was shaking her head, "this isn't how you can save me."

"Yes it is," I said, my own tears glistening in my eyes. I wasn't shoving them away this time.

"You honestly think that he's just going to let me go when you hit that inferno?" she said tearfully through the line.

She was trying to reason with me. I knew I had less than five minutes, but it felt like ages. The black mass of earth was becoming more and more defined. It was coming. My retribution. I licked my lips in anticipation. Maybe the scales would finally be balanced.

"No," she said. "No, Bas, what am I going to do without you?"

"Live a good life," I said harshly, though it wasn't directed at her.

I'd touched the outer rim of the gravity. There was no turning back now. The anticipation lifted the rhythm of my heart to a thicker, quicker beat. I could feel my blood pulsing, vibrating through my body. It would seem that as I finally wanted things to speed up they only slowed down. I looked at my dials going crazy now, swinging wildly out of control. Just like me. It was either this or let that bastard continue to hurt my sister and I wasn't going to let that happen.

"He's a monster, Bas," she insisted roughly. "There will be no one to enforce your stupid agreement if you're gone."

I didn't answer that. My thought process hadn't extended that far. No, I shook my head. I couldn't listen to her any more or she would dissuade me. I gripped the controller again. Don't loose faith, don't loose faith, I chanted over and over again in my head.

"Brother," she screamed. It took everything in me not to turn the stick and fly back to her.

"I have to do this, Bel," I said hoarsely. "He will kill you if I don't."

"No he won't. I'm his star. He won't touch me."

I snorted. "Do you think it was a fluke that you got through to me?"

"What... what do you mean?" she asked hesitantly.

She clearly hadn't thought about that.

"This is a test. He wants me to suffer in every way possible Bel, and I swear if there was a way for me to see you again I would, but there is a bomb in your room right now and it's timed so that it will go off a few seconds after I'm to hit the blaze if ..."

I couldn't finish the thought, the image too stark and horrible for me to fully contemplate.

"If you pull out, I blow," she finished quietly.

I nodded though there was no one to see it.

"He just wanted to hear me plead with you," she said, her rage returning.

"Yeah, Bel," I said, resigned. "Don't you see, this is the only way."

An overwhelming sense of sadness mixed with hatred swirled throughout my body, a mixture of both of our emotions.

"Bel," I said quietly.

"Yeah?"

She tried to answer evenly but I could hear the hitch in her voice.

"I love you and I'm so sorry."

"You have nothing to be sorry for."

"Yes, I do."

"No Bas. No you don't."

I tried to shake my head but the pod's rattling was so bad I didn't know if the bobbing of my chin was of my volition or not.

"It's because of me..." I started.

"Shhhhh," she said quietly. "We've all made mistakes. I slept with the bastard, not you."

"Yeah, true," I said, trying to keep it light. The tears were falling freely. "That was pretty stupid."

A strangled laugh came out of her and it mirrored my sentiments. I had less than a minute and that I would never see nor talk to her again finally hit me. That single bit of data was more horrifying and more detrimental to my final resolve than anything she could've said. My whole body ached and I knew she felt it when I heard a sniffle through the line. She was crying and she'd heard everything that I'd just thought. What an ass I was. After everything, I was putting even my last worry on her.

"Don't you dare do that," she said.

"Do what?" I asked weakly.

"Blame yourself for caring about me."

I wiped the tears from my cheeks and took a long, cleansing breath. I was seconds from my end. I was about to respond but the nose of my ship hit the blaze and whatever shielding I had was ripped away. The tin can became an inferno and I had no time left.

"I love you Bel," I said softly.

"I know you do big brother. Hey Bas?"

My ship was falling quickly into the fiery pit and my body suddenly burst into a blaze. I screamed and I felt panic overwhelm me. She was still connected to me in my mind.

No, Bel, get out of my head.

She didn't need to see this.

Bas, she called out wildly.

Go Bel, I yelled at her.

I will find you again. I promise.
It was the last thing I heard before I combusted, my final scream caught inside my death trap.

About Rhiannon Matlock

Born in 1981 before YouTube, Twitter or Twilight, Rhiannon Matlock remembers when you played your songs on Walkmans and actually had to tell your mother where you were going before you went out to play.

Now a well-seasoned traveler who still considers herself a child at heart Rhiannon enjoys such diverse activities as bungee jumping, white water rafting and volunteering in third world countries, but dislikes slow drivers and people who malign their friends.

Rhiannon doesn't like to talk about herself much, insisting that everyone else has a much more interesting story to tell. She especially likes to spin a good yarn, particularly ones where the white hat wins.

Connect with Rhiannon online:
rhiannonmatlock.wordpress.com
facebook.com/rhiannonmatlock

Other books by Rhiannon Matlock
On the Verge (Anthology)
Behind the Veil (Anthology)
The Death of Jimmy (Anthology)
Into the Abyss (Anthology)
Beyond the Threshold (Anthology)

Forgotten

By Laura Price

Like the fire in front of her, Amber's thoughts sway and flicker, reducing cognizance to ash. She stands, frozen, as great liquid tongues of fire lick up the foundation of her little ranch-style home. Ravenously they lap up the whitewashed walls, up the roof and further, in vain, to the sky. For Amber, the smoke is the voice of the tableau before her, telling the world that something is dying here. The dust, floating in chaos around her, remains as the only evidence that solidity had existed here, just moments before.

Her eyes feel glazed over as her mind plays a memory like a movie over the screen of flames. The smoke of the house-fire becomes the black clouds of a miserable day years before. She'd been working at Marizza's Boutique on the Boardwalk, staring out the window as a dark storm rolled in from the horizon. She'd forgotten her umbrella, but couldn't leave early to avoid the rain. The day before, she'd forgotten to come to work at all. Cathy, the owner, had been sweetly concerned, caring only for her safety since the "lapses" started happening. Cathy's understanding was a blessing and Amber wouldn't repay that by abandoning the store, even though it was empty.

Drenched in the downpour, she stood at the bus stop after work and barely noticed a man in a tan coat approach, holding a sky blue umbrella. He joined Amber in her gloomy vigil. Though hunched and shivering, she smiled vaguely up at him in greeting. When he smiled back, she saw a spark in his eye, which drew her out of her thoughts. He held his umbrella out toward her. "Pardon me, Ma'am. Would you mind holding this for me?"

"Of course," she had replied, but when she noticed that he was just standing there in the rain, she asked, laughing, if he wanted it back.

"Oh, no!" He waved his arms at her in warding. "Really,

my arm is so tired! If you would just hold it until the bus comes, I'd greatly appreciate it."

As she got to know him better, Amber found that Salus often did things like that. He left no room for argument, using an almost unwitting trickery to perform good deeds for people who would never allow him if asked. His ingenuity was so subtle that an observer wouldn't think to categorize him as intelligent. Salus didn't seem to plot, just move. The day that they had met, he hadn't wanted her phone number or a date, simply to cover a woman from the torrent of rain assailing her. In fact, it wasn't until the following week that she had asked him for his name and they began talking.

The weather that day was much nicer and even without the umbrella, she had recognized him immediately. He was plain, but not unhandsome, with black hair and a narrow face with soft brown eyes. Stepping off the bus at that same stop, she spotted him just as he walked into the old-timey burger joint, two doors down. Her decision to follow him was without debate and she smiled to herself for having caught the bus that made her forty minutes early instead of twenty minutes late.

As soon as she walked through the shiny red door of the restaurant, she saw him sitting alone at the bar. *Thank* God, she thought, he was smoking. As she walked up to him, she pulled out a long-awaited cigarette. "Excuse me, have you got a light?" she asked. She knew it wasn't the most titillating conversation starter, but it would have to do. "I always seem to lose mine."

He looked at her for a moment, thinking that he recognized her. "Sure." A smile curled up the left side of his mouth, and he swiveled the chair next to him around for her to sit in.

"I'm Amber," she smiled, probably blushing as she suddenly remembered that he had called her "ma'am" the last time they had spoken. "We met last week, in the rain." She pointed out the window toward the bus stop.

His eyes lit up, in that same way that had entranced her at the bus stop. He nodded and laughed, as they recalled the event. She felt incredibly comfortable with him, though they'd only just met. He was so full of life, yet just as his eyes had that spark, they also had a deep calmness that drew her in. To keep herself from staring, she absently glanced up at the clock and saw that she had two minutes to get to the store. Jumping up, and apologizing for being crazy, she managed to ask for his number while fumbling for a pen in her purse. When she made eye contact again with him, to hand him a business card, he looked quite amused. He clasped her hand in both of his, slowing her down enough to hear him, and promised to call her that evening.

In the years since, they had gotten married and bought the little house. Salus had painted it, as a surprise, during a weekend she'd spent away at her mother's. Not one piece of furniture was bought new, except for the mattresses. In the living room they had each received the calls and learned of the deaths of both of their fathers and the births of his nieces and nephew. The dining room had wood paneling that they both loved and would never renovate with drywall. They had, however, both agreed to remove the dark Autumn Leaves carpet and replace it with a brighter cream colored one.

In the bedroom, bathroom, up and down the hall, they'd paced through countless conversations about having babies. The conversation always ended with further travel plans and other obstacles to building a family. Amber had stopped taking birth-control, associating the hormone changes with her severe inability to concentrate. Salus hated using condoms with his own wife and argued that medicines had advanced and new options existed. Amber didn't like using condoms either, but she was scared and they couldn't deny that she hadn't had any of her lapses since she'd quit trying to find the "option" that would work for her. The small second bedroom existed as a well-used office space. In every room they had dreamed together, laughed, cried, and fought. Most often, they were happy.

First responders began to arrive, driving up the lawn and surrounding the house. They had taken a long time; she hadn't called them. They surround her, asking questions she can't understand, and move her toward a large white box with flashing lights. They sit her down, prod her and shine lights in her eyes. Their voices are a distant and meaningless sound. For a moment, she almost gets an impression that she should try to focus on them, but she can't see them. She sees only the flame and the black sky.

It was only an hour ago that she had come home, on her lunch break, to check on Salus. He'd stayed home sick with a fever and headache. She had quietly tip-toed inside, stopping to stare at his serenely sleeping form, curled up in a comforter on the sofa. The morning paper laid in a pyramid-like shambles on the coffee table, next to a bottle of cough syrup, a pile of tissues, and her new birth control pills. He'd found them, and was undoubtedly happy, although she'd planned to surprise him.

Reaching down to brush a wisp of hair off his forehead, he suddenly seemed to drift further away from her. Her vision frosted around the edges, increasing as he drifted deeper into the center, until she no longer recognized him. She looked in every direction, trying to comprehend her surroundings, while panic grew inside her. She fought for each breath as her heart started racing. Her chest burned. The living room walls, the furniture, everything around her seemed both far away, yet too close as she tried to grasp where she was.

She spun around and around trying to find something she could recognize, knowing there must be an answer for why she was there. She saw shapes and textures, but the connection to names and functions were gone. She couldn't place the purpose of the oven mitts lying on the kitchen counter. A collectable spoon rack, made by Salus, in the shape of the United States, seemed menacing as the silver mementoes shone incongruently in the darkness. She felt mocked by a set of encyclopedias, not realizing they had been her mother's; their intelligence had helped raise her. Then, the spinning panic in her mind stopped and went blank with a deafening silence. She knew what she must do.

Amber looked down, calmly, at the sleeping stranger. Not a line of worry creased his face. He was innocent. She resolved to allow him this peaceful rest.

"I'll fix this," she whispered almost silently, petting aside a loose strand of hair from his forehead.

She picked up the newspaper, the bottle of cold medicine, this month's Cosmo. A glass of water stood like a sentinel in the center of the end table. As she reached for it, light from the window hit the puddle of condensation around its base, glistening brightly in the dim room. Shielding her eyes against it, she moved on, unnerved, grabbing a painting of pine trees off the dining room wall, her house-warming gift to Salus, and the oven mitts. Squinting in fear, she took down the collectible spoons rack. With a match from a box advertising her favorite restaurant, she lit the gas stove and piled on the myriad debris of her home. The fire burned her as it grew, continuously forcing her to step farther back. Finally pushed outside, off the porch and into the yard, she noticed the silver Lancer sitting in the driveway stupidly. She left its justice to the fire, watching as the flames reached out toward it, too.

Lifting her into the ambulance, the paramedics are still speaking incoherently to her. The fire fighters douse a 1200 square foot pile of soot with their powerful hoses. *What had stood there before?* She tries to remember.

About Laura Price

Laura Price is the imaginary person behind the eyes of her favorite character. She has had multiple short stories and poetry published, and is always filing little pieces of life in her mind to be later threaded into a new web. She lives in her own personal paradise on the beaches of Florida, where she works, plays, writes, and raises her prodigal progeny. Providing care and council for patients, Laura's work revolves around human interaction and conflict resolution. The subtle connections between people present a sort of magic which is the greatest inspiration to her writing.

Connect with Laura online:
www.AuthorLauraPrice.com
twitter.com/AuthorLPrice
facebook.com/laura.price

Other books by Laura Price
On the Verge (Anthology)
Behind the Veil (Anthology)
The Death of Jimmy (Anthology)

Thank you for taking the time to enjoy our creative works. Look out for more books from the Ink Slingers Guild, both as a group and as individuals!

If you enjoyed any or all of the stories in this book, we would love it if you could take a few minutes to share it on Amazon or Goodreads. Your opinion really does make a difference!

May your world be filled with adventure and the stuff that dreams are made of.

Cheers!

The Ink Slingers Guild

www.InkSlingersGuild.com